OVERWHELMING ACCLAIM FOR *OUT OF BODY*

"Compelling, memorable . . . one of the best reads I've had in years."
>—Harry Crews, author of *Body*, *Scar Lover* and *A Feast of Snakes*

"Calls to mind Truman Capote's *In Cold Blood* in its depiction of the outsider in American society, in an intriguing blend of the realistic and the hallucinatory."
>—Avery Corman, author of *Kramer Vs. Kramer* and *Prized Possessions*

"An unusual story of a decent guy not at home in his own body, thanks to a family secret too hideous to imagine. Reminiscent of the parry and punch of Jim Thompson."
>—Darryl Ponicsan, author of *The Last Detail*

"Tom Baum's work has the elegant eeriness of a vision."
>—Chandler Brossard, author of *The Bold Saboteurs*

"OUT OF BODY grabbed me with steel fingers."
>—Marshall Brickman, co-writer of *Annie Hall* and *Manhattan*

More . . .

OUT OF BODY

THOMAS BAUM

St. Martin's Paperbacks

OUT OF BODY

Copyright © 1997 by Thomas Baum.

Library of Congress Catalog Card Number: 96-52646

ISBN: 0-312-96735-7

Printed in the United States of America

St. Martin's Press hardcover edition/May 1997
St. Martin's Paperbacks edition/July 1999

10 9 8 7 6 5 4 3 2 1

For Carol, Henry, and Will.
And for Keri Isbell.

*And he shall be filled
with the Holy Ghost,
even from his mother's womb.*

LUKE 1:15

PART ONE

1

Five minutes into my parole hearing, despite all Carl Williams's warnings, I started to drift.

I was staring at the library walls, answering questions, more or less on auto, thinking about what Carl had said, how the walls of institutions were painted green because looking at grass and trees is supposed to be good for the soul, except if you're inside a prison, or a school for that matter, or a hospital or funny farm, green reminds you how evil you are, how ignorant, sick, or crazy. The reforms of one generation are the problems of the next—that was one of my dad's sayings, not Carl's.

And so by and by I lost the thread.

"Can you explain the circumstances?"

I snapped to. "Of what, sir?"

"The two fights. And the one that landed you in solitary."

"Okay. The other man's name is Carl Williams. He's a friend on my cellblock, he's a block leader. Can I speak frankly, sir? I know Carl wouldn't mind."

"That's what we're here for, Mr. Hake." Fortunately or not, my guy's mind was somewhere else—

he was thumbing through the other cases he had coming up today.

I said, "Carl had just lost a buddy to parole. He was testing me, and I misread his intentions."

"Did you think his intentions were sexual?"

"No, sir. I wasn't sure, I had to draw the line. As I say, we're friends now. He's African-American."

My guy looked at me over his clipboard. "I didn't ask his race," he said.

"Yes, sir," I said. That's how hard I was spacing—I'd forgotten, for the moment, that my guy was black. "I'm saying, if you check the dates, both those infractions occurred in the first six months. Otherwise, I believe my record is spotless."

He gave me a narrow look. "In the board's experience, the best prisoners can make the worst citizens."

"I hope to be a good citizen," I said.

"You're not a stupid man, Mr. Hake."

"No, sir. I hope not."

"Middle-class background."

"Yes, sir."

"Your parents? What do they do?"

I must have hesitated, because the other two board members—a chinless lady with a parrot beak, and a guy in shirtsleeves with a bullet-shaped head—looked up from their paperwork. "My dad was a doctor," I said. "Internal medicine."

"How much schooling did *you* have?"

"High-school degree. One year of community college."

"And one juvenile arrest for shoplifting."

"Yes, sir."

"What jobs have you held?"

I looked at the wall above his head—green.

"In here? First I worked in the mess hall. Then here in the law library. Outside, I've been a clerk, a carpenter, fry cook, housepainter."

"And you worked in a sporting-goods store."

He said this loud, for the benefit of the other two board members. They were shuffling through their own cases, trying to figure out which of the guys sitting behind me belonged to them. My mouth was drying up fast.

"Yes, sir. I sold sporting goods."

"You didn't see fit to mention that."

"No, sir," I said. I heard my teeth click together—a trait of my mom's.

"Assuming you're granted parole," he said, "where do you plan on living?"

"My family," I said.

"With your mother and father?"

"My dad passed away," I said—I was trying to relax my jaw. "With my brother," I said. And his wife, I started to say, then thought better of it. Parrot Lady was listening now. "And temping in his office. I believe he wrote you to that effect."

"He may have," said my guy, without bothering to check.

"I have a car," I blurted.

"I beg your pardon?"

"I own a car. My brother garaged it for me." They always want to know about your car—as Carl put it, they don't want to picture you on foot. "My brother sells insurance. Owns his own company."

My guy stared at me coldly through his horn-rims.

"Your caseworker, you probably know, has recommended parole. Otherwise you wouldn't be here."

"Actually, I believe it was Reverend Dalton. He took over my case."

"You didn't get along with your caseworker?"

Careful, I thought. "I think he found my bitterness hard to swallow. The chaplain, on the other hand, helped me get past my resentments. My mom's a religious woman, she instilled that in me as well."

They were all staring at me now, Bullet Head, Parrot Lady, my guy. "Bitter about what? Why would you be bitter?"

Don't let them retry the case, Carl warned me. If you start to lose focus, that's what they'll do.

"He believes in God's plan, and he helped me to believe in it."

"And if you're not granted parole? Will that shake your faith?"

"Sir, I hope not."

"You hope not," said my guy.

Parrot Lady cleared her throat. "Denton," she said, in a gentle voice, "do you plan to attend church if you're paroled?"

"Yes, ma'am," I said eagerly. Things were blurring out, blackening around the edges. It was like I was looking at my guy through a paper-towel core. Parrot Lady was reaching past him for my file.

"Do you know where Sandra Loyacano is living?" he said.

"No, sir. She was living in Spokane."

My guy and Bullet Head were trading looks. I glanced behind me, half-expecting to see the girl I was supposed to have raped sitting there surrounded by her relatives, and the guy who wrote me up for the Spokane paper, and the judge who pronounced sentence, and the mayor of the town where I was proposing to live—of course there were only other inmates, waiting their turn.

"Oh but you *did* know her address," my guy said.

"No. No, sir. Not the exact address." I tried to turn my mind off, keep his voice from leaking in.

"She came into the sporting-goods store."

"Yes, sir. She bought hand-weights." Keep your damn mouth shut—I couldn't.

"She wrote you out a check, her address was on the check."

Suddenly I was picturing Sandra Loyacano, the lizard tattoo on her thigh.

"She pulled you out of a lineup."

"Yes, I know," I said, "because she saw me in the store." I could hear the heat in my voice, I could feel my lips moving.

"When you talked to the police, they asked you to describe her. You identified her by her tattoo. She wasn't naked in the store, was she?"

God help me, I was back in the courtroom. "Sir, no. Except maybe in the changing room."

"You followed her home, you watched as she punched out the alarm code, jacked open the French doors, robbed her in broad daylight."

I could picture it all, the way you picture something when you read about it. "No, sir," I said.

My guy adjusted his horn-rims.

"All right," he said. "As I say, I think we don't want to rehash this now."

"Thank you, sir." My hairline was getting wet—I could hear myself talking, but it was like I was in the next room. I could see myself through their eyes, and it was not a pretty sight.

"You pleaded guilty to robbery and felony assault."

"On advice of counsel. He said he couldn't beat the state's case." I wet my lips. "I couldn't afford a long trial, my brother didn't have the money. They made me a one-time offer.''

I was waiting for him to say it, for Parrot Lady's edification: they found my pubic hair in her sheets. "You had no alibi," was all he said, however.

"Yes, sir. That's why a deal was cut. May I say something, sir?" Here I go, I thought. "I know you want me to express remorse. If I had done what I was accused of doing—never tried for, but accused—I would feel remorse, because guilty or not, I believe I'm one of those people that prison can help. I could never rape anyone," I insisted, raising my eyes from my lap, "that's why I accepted a plea bargain. I knew my luck was going south and I didn't want that stain on my record. And now I find it's there anyhow." I glanced over at Parrot Lady, who gave me a tight little smile, sympathy, hostility, I couldn't tell which. "I know you'd prefer I came clean, having realized the error of my ways, because then I would be a credit to the prison system, instead of what you seem to think I am, a loose cannon and a rapist and a psychopathic liar. Well, I'm none of those things.''

Except a loose cannon, at that moment for sure.

"Mr. Hake, did we say anything about rape?"

I saw Parrot Lady's face fall—she closed my file, pushed it back at my guy. I felt like I was sitting in midair.

"I think we can wrap this up," my guy said.

"I want to say something else," I said.

"Go ahead, Denton." It was Parrot Lady.

I was in freefall. "I never had any trouble finding women."

"That will be all, Mr. Hake."

"Yes, sir. I want to thank the board for their patience," I said.

"Goodbye, Mr. Hake."

My entire body twitched. It was like I had fallen asleep and now suddenly woke up, slamming into the mattress like a stunt man, dropped there from the high green ceiling. There was a guard outside my cell, grinning like he'd bet his salary check against me—when my cell door clanged shut, it felt like the very first time.

2

That feeling stayed with me for a week. I was back in time, reliving those first dead days after the curiosity wore off, after the first crying jags—if I closed my eyes the ceiling was an inch above my head. All those guys now getting out before me—I couldn't stand thinking about them, guys who were doing three years for armed robbery, incest, whatever, and me looking at another four. Four more years! I'd leave here a worthless piece of shit, fit for nothing but another stretch.

I didn't call my brother Elliot. He said to contact him after the hearing, tell him how it went, but I didn't want to upset Mom. As for Carl Williams, he was sick in the infirmary, food allergy, so just as the shock was wearing off I had to go through it all again for him.

"I told you to focus, didn't I?"

Carl was stacking books in the library—I was trying to read up on my rights, whether I was entitled to a look at my records. "My guy had it in for me."

He gaped at me with his bloodshot eyes. "Bullshit, Denton, you always assume the worst. It's like you're applying for a loan—it doesn't matter what you said or what you think you said or how you came across.

Maybe you get five points off for demeanor, maybe not, I wasn't there. The facts are, you got a family to come home to, your brother owns his own home, you got a car, job prospects, you're the first in your family to do time, it all adds up."

There was a patch of blue in the library window, and what looked like a vapor trail, and while Carl lectured me I was dreaming myself into the sky, watching the prison slide quietly away beneath me. Then suddenly I was back—I felt my fist slam into the wall.

"Hey," said the guard by the door.

Carl gripped me by the wrist. "Did you hear one word I just said?"

"It's like a loan application," I said. That was the last thing I remembered.

"Where were you just now?"

"Someplace else," I said. This was Topic One with Carl, my tendency to float away under pressure. "Up there," I added sheepishly, nodding toward the ceiling.

"How bad did you space out in front of the board?"

"Bad."

"How bad?"

"I started blabbing about rape."

Carl groaned. "What did I tell you."

"I know. I lost it."

"You didn't rape that girl."

"I told them that," I said.

"You didn't tell them you were tripping at the time."

"*No*," I said. "I said I wasn't capable of rape."

"You weren't convicted of rape."

"I know," I said.

"You're getting out! Picture it!"

What I saw was the inside of my cell. I pictured myself as a kid, and if I had a crystal ball, and could see myself now, locked up, what would I think, what would I do, would I have gotten into trouble sooner in life, would I have bothered finishing high school, would I have blown my brains out. I tried thinking Carl had some special knowledge of my fate, but two more days and no word from the parole board, and the bitterness washed over me with a vengeance. At meals and in the rec room, guys started ragging me.

"Denton, do you believe in prayer?"

People knew I never missed chapel—I took a lot of shit for it, especially from T. Rex and Lloyd, two rednecks who resented Carl's power on the wing.

"Yes," I said. "I'm praying you go away."

"Betting is a form of prayer," said Lloyd. "According to your girlfriend."

"*I'm* betting you get out," said T. Rex. He had triangular teeth, huge spaces between, and a hole in the bridge of his nose big enough for a third eye. He took my pinky in his fingers and started to wiggle it. "Because anyone could see you're a no-threat pussy."

I yanked my hand away. "Do me a favor," I said.

"If we knew you wasn't leaving," said Lloyd, "we'd leave you alone."

The rec room was emptying out, there was no guard in sight. Lloyd was stroking his chin whiskers. "Don't be looking around for Carl. Carl ain't here."

"That nigger bet *against* you, did you know that, babyface? He gave me five to one you weren't gonna make parole."

"He's jealous, dude. He ain't getting out no time

soon, and he can't stand to part with you.''

I tried to get up—they both held me down.

"Come on, genius, we want to see if you're a real blonde.''

Somebody flowed out of my body, something flowed in. Lloyd was taking down his pants.

"When you suck that nigger's dick tonight," said T. Rex, "guess whose face you're gonna see.''

The next thing I knew he was screaming in pain. I saw myself grab his head by the ears and slam it into the bench. I wanted to tap myself on the shoulder, tell myself to stop—suddenly I felt my arms being wrenched behind my back. Two guards were wrestling me into the hallway.

"What the fuck are you doing, Hake? What do you think this is, Senior Week?''

They threw me in my cell, banned me from everything but meals. I tried to sleep but I couldn't, just lay there staring up through my eyelids at the ceiling, picturing the next four years, hassles every week until they were forced to transfer me, which of course would go on my record and become the main item at my next parole hearing. At breakfast I could hardly open my mouth to speak. Carl didn't care, he was chattering away as usual.

"—You want to know why you're a pessimist?''

I was watching T. Rex and Lloyd. They were plotting something new.

"You loved your dad, right?'' Carl's bloodshot eyes bulged at me. I realized he'd been talking for several minutes.

"I didn't know him that well," I said. "I was young.''

"You loved him," he told me. "Try and think about that.''

I tried, but all I could picture was his nurse, Dot, how she used to stroke my hair like she owned me. "So?"

"And he shot himself, and now nothing can ever work out for you."

I looked at him dimly. "Simple as that," I said.

He lowered his voice. "Let's say you don't get your parole."

"Yeah, let's say."

"We'll bust out together. I promise you. First— you listening?—we get us reassigned to the kitchen."

That's when I knew I was doomed to do my full eight years. "I never broke any law," I said, "what the fuck is going on, this life is fucked—" and on and on in that vein. "They did this to me, they made me into this, I never hated the world like this, never—"

"When your dad killed himself? I bet you did. I bet you were scared then too. Abandoned by fate? Think about it. You've been tripping ever since."

I was so sunk in my own misery I couldn't move. Carl was just sitting there, too, silent, wise, and help-less.

"You'll be all right," he kept saying.

I might as well get used to it, I thought. No more pretending I didn't belong here. I took a bite—my stomach flew up to meet the food.

"Aw shit," I heard somebody say. I managed to throw up in my hand and gulp most of it back.

When I got back to my cell, they were slipping an envelope under my door.

Carl saw it before I did.

"Shit," he said.

He was grinning. I didn't get it.

"It's fat, you dumb motherfucker."

There were four pages, three copies. *CONDITIONS OF PAROLE.* I sat down on my bed, I couldn't stand, my hands were trembling. *Willingness to change . . . Additional prison time will do no good and probable harm . . . Not to contact the victim, Sandra Loyacano . . . Will enter a community-based therapy program.* Then a parole officer's name: *ORTEGA, FELIX.*

"What it is," said Carl solemnly, "they're cranking up the war on drugs again, they need the beds."

I sat there reading my release, stunned and happy. "Thank God for crime," I said.

"Yeah, we'd all be in here forever." We went out to the yard—I went around paying off my poker debts, while Carl sat by himself watching me. I was starting to feel sorry for him.

"The best thing about it—now I don't have to bust you out of here." We were back in my cell, he was trying to act cheerful. "That's gonna make it so much easier for me. Where you gonna be, Tacoma?"

"Auburn. At my brother's."

"Even better. I used to work for a guy in Auburn. Lefcourt Construction. Write it down, you'll forget it."

I wrote it down.

"He's always hiring, doesn't ask too many questions. When exactly do you leave?"

"Thursday," I said.

He started taking off his T-shirt. "Then it's time to cash in my chips."

I must have been dreading this moment, in the privacy of my mind, because I just sat there staring.

"What did you think, you were getting all that protection for free?"

Jesus, I thought, this isn't happening.

''I guess your word don't mean shit,'' he said.

''What word?''

''What word. You don't remember a fucking thing that happens, do you, Hake? You been someplace else the whole time.''

''Carl,'' I said, ''this is bullshit.''

''Thursday, is that the date they gave you? That's three days from now. Still time for T. Rex and Lloyd to have their way with you. Shame if you left here in a shoebox.'' His eyes were bloodshot and dancing. I was thinking of how much I owed him. I pictured him holding me in his arms, like it was something I'd chosen to forget.

''All right,'' I said. ''Just someplace where nobody's gonna see us.''

Carl looked at me. Then he waved his hand in front of my face.

''Denton, you're tripping out again.''

It was true. I could feel myself slipping away, floating toward the ceiling, like I was planning to watch us in the act. Then I felt Carl's hand on my knee.

''I never asked. You never promised.''

''All right,'' I said, relieved.

''You're not a faggot *or* a rapist.''

''If you say so,'' I said.

He slapped my shoulder. He barked with laughter. ''I tell you what you *can* do,'' he said. ''Leave me your sunblock, I'll jerk off to your sweet ass.''

''Suit yourself,'' I said sourly. I was thinking about my dad, how he used to thumb-wrestle with me and my brother Elliot for hours, laughing gleefully every time he won, which of course was all the time. I looked up from the floor and there was the guard with my parole papers—fear shot through me like a drug. It was all a joke, it was all a mistake!

"Shit," I said under my breath.

"What is it now?" said Carl.

The guard snapped the papers at me.

"You didn't sign them, numbnuts."

"Oh yeah," I said.

They were both looking at me, both shaking their heads.

"Oh yeah," said Carl.

3

Maybe they did need the cell, because they let me out a day early. My brother Elliot was supposed to come for me on Thursday, but when Wednesday came they called me out after breakfast and told me to report to checkout.

I asked if I could say goodbye to Carl.

"Sure," said the desk guy. "Come back during visiting hours."

That's how I knew I was free. They gave me my goody bag, $126.50 in gate money, a pair of khakis, a polyester work shirt, thin black socks—somebody must have worked a deal, they were all from the same store. Also a condom from some government program, plus my wallet, penknife, everything I came in with, my driver's license, still valid, my old apartment key.

I caught a ride into Walla Walla with the laundry truck. In the Greyhound terminal I changed into my new clothes, called my brother's machine and told him they let me out already, if he got home before seven I could sure use a ride from the Tacoma station, otherwise I'd grab a taxi. Elliot's outgoing message was new, with an option to leave a message for his wife Mimi. That jarred me—a Rip Van Winkle

moment, Carl had warned me about those, and soon
they were coming thick and fast. For example, in the
coffee bar—the girls' voices all sounded alike, they
could have been from anywhere. There was something in the air, less smog, something dirtier than
smog, unless this was just my fucked-up mood. Girls'
lips looked bigger and the cars all looked the same,
with their butts in the air, all trying to look Japanese.
I'd noticed some of this on TV but it wasn't the
same. After boarding I rested my forehead against the
window and watched the bus shadow skate over the
weeds on the highway. Everybody was pumping their
own gas. The buildings, the ones that looked like the
architects played with too many Legos, they looked
old. The faces in the street were darker, fearful, full
of geeky looks—that much I could tell from TV, too.
Some insect thing had happened—Carl said it was
the Cold War being over, everything up for grabs
now, a smell in the air, like gasoline, a whole feeling
to the free world now that you couldn't sense from
the TV shows they let us watch or the magazines they
let us read.

The ride through the Washington desert went
smoothly. I was fairly calm, not too jumpy, staying
within myself, though my muscles felt tentative, like
after a cold. Then in Ellensburg we made a pit stop
outside a convenience store, and I almost got caught
in a hassle. A guy came in the door, logger type in
grunge clothes, saying, "You the blue Taurus?"

I had no idea he was talking to me.

"It's blocking my truck," he said.

"I said it's not my car," I said. I hadn't said anything, I just didn't like his tone.

"All right." He backed off. "Don't get your pant-
ies in a twist," he said.

"Hey," I said. Suddenly I felt like the day before my parole came through, a little jolt from the depths, the unfairness of it all, black adrenaline pounding behind my eyes. I watched myself follow him out to the lot, got within ten feet of the guy before I turned myself around. Easy does it, I heard myself say, and got back on the bus. I could see there were these moments to watch out for.

Tacoma wasn't the Tacoma I remembered—it was part of the Anywhere now. I called Elliot from the bus station. This time I got his wife, Mimi, live, and introduced myself.

"Yes, of course. Hello. We got your message."

She had a voice like honey but she sounded bummed. "I'm a day ahead of schedule," I told her. "I can take a cab."

"No, Denton, your brother's on his way." I heard a dog barking in the background, I could hear the tension in her voice. Elliot hated dogs, so I knew the dog wasn't his. I said goodbye and hung up.

Ten minutes later, Elliot's Camry pulled into the lot.

I didn't move from the bench, and he didn't see me at first. I sat there watching my brother go up to the ticket seller to ask when my bus was due. I was scared to see him, so scared and so glad I couldn't breathe for a second—my throat closed up and I started to cough. Then I had to ease myself off the bench so he wouldn't know I'd been sitting there the whole time.

He saw me coming toward him and we hugged.

"Oh my," he said.

"Yeah," I said. "Here I am."

He was wearing a white shirt and tie and he looked ten years older, balding now, eyeglasses. For a second I thought I saw Mom in the front seat of the Camry, but it was only the headrest. Elliot said, as we got into the car, "Mom might not be by tonight." The old fraternal ESP. My heart sank.

"It's hard for her," he said.

The road climbed until the houses thinned out, split levels among evergreens. Every house had a private security sign, and these weren't even mansions. Elliot had the radio up loud.

"What's Mimi doing now? I know you wrote me."

"She's still a decorator," he said. "She's going for her real estate license."

"Good for her," I said. For most of the ride Elliot was quiet, and that bothered me. We used to ride around our home town, saying nothing and not minding it, cruising for girls, listening to the radio, and now I felt his silence right down to my toes.

"You oughta check these guys out, they're good, Pearl Jam," he said at last.

"I know," I said. The Camry was pulling up at his new house. "We had radios."

"Of course you did. Sorry."

"No problem," I said, checking out the house. It was a big red barn with a garage out back. Elliot let me go in first, called Mimi's name. The living room had a giant plaster eagle on the wall, two big rocking chairs, and huge pillows with Presidents' faces.

"I feel like the Shrinking Man," I said.

Elliot held a finger to his lips. Evidently Mimi was the decorator and she might be hiding someplace, watching me from the shadows, the way I'd spied on Elliot at the bus station. The table was set for four, but with three wine glasses. Somewhere a dog was barking.

"Mimi!"

Elliot was getting annoyed.

"I'll go up to the garage," I said, "freshen up."

"No, I want you to meet her," said Elliot in a clipped voice. His ears were turning red. "Mimi, he's here!"

Nothing happened, and then a door opened, their bedroom, and Mimi came out—five foot six and no more than a hundred pounds, cigarette in her fingers, wearing a white shirt over a green leotard and a tense smile.

"Mimi, this is Denton."

I started toward her, realizing I was about to touch a woman's flesh for the first time in four years— suddenly the dog bounded in from the bedroom, barking up a storm. Elliot was shooshing it, she wasn't.

"Well, who's this?" I said to the dog.

"This is Ozzie," said Mimi tightly. The dog kept barking as I put out my hand—she waited a second before she shook it. "Ozzie, off," she said, with a glance at the government-issue bag I was carrying. "Elliot, show Denton his room, I still have to wash the lettuce."

She stayed rooted to the spot till I was out the back door. Elliot put a key in my hand and pointed toward the garage—the next moment he was back in the kitchen, chewing her out for acting so cold. I walked past my old Chevy Nova, up the stairs, unlocked the door. There were two rooms plus a bath, Elliot's sofa from before his marriage in the main room, my old bed and night table in the tiny bedroom area, and some of Mom's artwork, the mosaics of famous paintings she used to make out of plastic coffee spoons. I checked out the bureau—some PJs, some

T-shirts, some of my old clothes, a picture of Elliot with Mom and a picture of Mom alone, and a Gideon Bible with gold lettering. Nothing of Dad's at all, of course—most of that was long gone, sold or burned. The main room had a homey redwood smell—there was a microwave, a baby fridge, a potted fern, a phone, an answering machine, my old TV, a nice view of the house and the yard, and because the garage was on a rise, a view of the street beyond, with its twin rows of pines.

Mom's Riviera was pulling up in front.

All of a sudden I didn't want to be there. I didn't want Mom to see me yet, not till I was on better terms with Mimi, because of how that would hurt Mom, to see how much fear her son inspired. I watched her come up the front walk—I was glued to the spot. When I sat down on the bed I felt like I was back in prison, letting myself drift off until I couldn't feel the floor under my shoes. I was floating up the driveway, feet barely touching the asphalt, flying inches above the ground—the next thing I knew I was walking across the backyard, trying to get a grip, my face tingling like I'd just splashed water on it. Probably I had—my forehead was still damp.

I tiptoed into the house.

Mom was in the kitchen, pouring dressing on the salad. When she saw me she dropped the salad spoon—she threw her arms around me. For a second we just held each other.

"Look at you," she said.

I lifted her off the ground and she giggled. Her face was thinner, darker, suntanned, her neck flesh was looser, and now I realized she'd cut her hair short. She caught sight of my black socks, felt the lapel of my shirt.

"Where'd you get these?" she said, and didn't wait for an answer—she was searching my face. "So the government finally came to their senses."

Behind her back, I saw Elliot give Mimi a look—Mom laced her fingers through mine, walking me out of the kitchen.

"My goodness, you came out handsome. How are you feeling?"

"Better now you're here."

She hugged me again, and Mimi called us to sit down—mine was the place without the wine glass. Elliot started to drink his soup and Mom made a tut-tut noise, so Elliot put down his spoon and said grace. For a long time nobody spoke, then Elliot started in on current events, taking pains to let Mimi know I was up on most things, I hadn't just crawled out of a cave. I could tell how anxious he was for her to like me, and she was trying her best, so was everybody, and I felt myself lighten, I felt my heart rise as if I were looking in through the window from the street outside, seeing a normal happy family with an average amount of history, chatting away like we were all interested in each other.

"So what are you selling a lot of?" I was saying.

"Earthquake insurance," Elliot said. "And we're nowhere near a fault line."

"How about major medical for dogs?" I said, glancing at Ozzie. "I hear that's a trend."

"The people in this town are half-nutty," said Mom. She patted my hand. "But you're going to love it here, isn't he, Mimi?"

Mimi looked up from her plate. "I'm sorry?" She was spacing out in *her* way, whatever that was.

"I said, we're gonna try and help him all we can, aren't we?"

Mimi gave Elliot a help-me look. Ozzie, who'd been lying the whole time by Mimi's chair, went on alert. "I thought that's what we were doing," Mimi said.

Mom's coffee cup clanked down. "Okay," she said fiercely. "I want a show of hands."

"Mom, take it easy," I said.

"Now that we're all together. How many people thought Denton was guilty?"

"Mom, for Christ's sake," said Elliot.

"Don't curse at me, Elliot. I asked a question."

"It's okay, Mom," I said. "Don't do this." I looked straight at Mimi. "I never raped that girl," I told her.

At first Mimi didn't respond, just sneaked another look at Elliot—she must have been thinking of my hairs in Sandra Loyacano's sheets, the cash in my pocket that supposedly came out of her bag, unless of course Elliot had never spoken of these things to Mimi. I was hoping that was true, and then Mimi spoke up again.

"That you remember," she said in a tight voice, almost a'whisper. She reached for a cigarette and lit it with her old one. Mom looked around at everybody like she couldn't believe what she was hearing.

"There is nothing wrong with Denton's memory," she declared.

For a moment the table was silent. "Is that why you didn't give me a wine glass?" I said to Mimi. "You thought I was having blackouts?"

"I only know what I've been told," said Mimi.

"And what have you been told?" said Mom.

Mimi tried to back off. "I thought parolees weren't supposed to drink."

"Denton is a dreamer," Mom insisted, "and that's

all. Absentminded professor, always pretending he was someplace else, as far back as we can remember.''

''Since Dad died,'' said Elliot, and promptly got up from the table. ''I'll help you clear,'' he said to Mimi, who was halfway into the kitchen. I got up from the table too, and the next thing I knew Mom was heading for the front door.

''Denton, walk me to the car.''

I started to protest, but she was out the door— Elliot and Mimi were jawing at each other in the kitchen, and I was bolting into the night after Mom.

''I'm having trouble warming up to that woman,'' she said.

''Really?'' I said lightly. ''It doesn't show.''

''*She's* the drinker,'' said Mom. ''Not you.''

''Why don't you go back and say thank you?''

''I said goodbye, didn't you hear me?''

''Yes,'' I said. I did remember now.

''She made Elliot quit the church, did he tell you that?''

''No,'' I said. And then in hopes of making her feel better, I said, ''I was thinking of joining myself.''

''He does everything she tells him. He'll do anything to make that marriage work. He'd rather have a happy marriage than be happy,'' she said, taking out her keys.

I could feel Elliot's eyes on us—sure enough, when I glanced back I saw he was watching us out the front window. ''Then he took a chance inviting me to live here,'' I said. ''I'm sure Mimi never bargained on that.''

''He wants to keep an eye on you,'' said Mom. ''He loves you, too, you know.''

"I know he does," I said.

"Trying every way he knows not to be his father. It breaks my heart." She squeezed my hand earnestly—her eyes were misting over. "When a man takes his life, the Devil curses his children."

We were cursed before, I thought, but I didn't want to split hairs.

"God sees the truth, even if other people don't. God was testing you, Denny, that's why He sent you to prison for no reason."

I put my arm around her. "Mom, if your battery goes dead, you think God is testing you."

"Go on, laugh at me. I had the battery replaced," she said, unlocking her Riviera. "Now don't feel you have to come and see me, I'm not crazy about visitors anyhow. Elliot has me over every Wednesday. Friday's their night to make love, so be warned. They're trying to make a baby, could you sense that?"

"No," I said.

"To keep the marriage together," she said, slamming the car door. I leaned in and kissed her through the open window.

"Goodbye, hon," she said.

I watched her car until it disappeared, thinking back to the nights Dad brought his nurse, Dot, home to dinner, along about the time they started their affair, and how Mom always had to cook her best dishes. As for Elliot and Mimi, they were back in the living room now—her shoes were off and he was massaging her feet, so rather than intrude I went up the driveway to the garage. I was looking through my things, the clothes of mine they'd put in the bureau, when Elliot knocked on the door and let himself in. He was carrying a coffee-maker—I watched him plug it in.

"What did Mom say to you?" he said.

He moved past me to the window, untangling the blinds. "She said you're not going to church anymore."

"She doesn't approve of Mimi."

I couldn't lie to Elliot, so I didn't deny it. "She said you're trying to get pregnant," I said. And I added, "Congratulations."

"Is that what Mom told you?"

"Yes," I said. "Why, isn't it true?"

He didn't answer. "You wouldn't believe her house," he said.

"What about it?"

"The basement. She put everything back like it was."

"Why?" I said.

He scraped a hand through his hair. "The Suicide Museum." For a while I didn't say anything—he was staring out the window at the backyard like it didn't belong to him, like he was remembering our old backyard. I came and stood next to him, picturing the wisteria, and the part of the lawn that turned into a lake after a heavy rain, remembering how we used to play catch in the dark, and how once a year Dad used to come out and throw the ball around with us, whether we wanted him to or not. That always pissed Elliot off, which puzzled me at the time—but of course he knew things I never saw.

I moved away from the window. "Where'd she get the gold-lettered Bible?" I asked.

"Sands Hotel, Las Vegas," he said. He drummed his fingers on the glass. "About your work situation," he said.

He looked worried. "I got a lead on a job," I said.

"Where?"

"From a friend," I said.

"In prison?"

"He used to work in Auburn—Lefcourt Construction, ever hear of it?"

He shook his head. "I wouldn't count on anything you heard in prison," he said stiffly. "I would try to leave all that behind. Unfortunately, there's no temp work right now," he said. "And all our runners have to be bonded. I talked it over with Mimi," he said, gazing back at the yard, "and she agreed we could pay you for jobs around the house, till you find something."

"Thank you," I said. I tried to sound grateful, but it didn't come out that way. I wanted the Lefcourt thing to work out, for Carl's sake.

"She'll tell you what she wants done. Meanwhile," he said, and he reached into his shirt pocket, "you can open up an account with this."

It was a check for five hundred dollars, written on their joint account, Elliot Hake and Mimi Cotter Hake.

"By the way," he said, "that's your own phone line."

"Elliot, I do appreciate all this."

He started out the door and stopped.

"Was it hell in there?"

At first I thought he meant at dinner, then I realized he was talking about prison. "Yeah, now and then."

He nodded. "Lotta animals. Lotta Dull Normals."

I was surprised to hear him use this term—Dull Normal was one of Dad's expressions, and Elliot had tried to purge himself of those. "I never got raped, if that's what you were wondering," I said.

He only shrugged, and I wished I hadn't used the

word rape. "Did you space out a lot? I imagine you did."

"I had a guy looking after me." And I smiled. "Like you look after me," I said.

That seemed to satisfy him. "Good night, Denny," he said. "I'm glad you're here, because we love you."

"I know that," I said.

"Good night," he said.

I watched him walk back to the house. Pretty soon the light in the living room went off and the bedroom light came on. I could see them in the bathroom, Mimi putting cold cream on her face, Elliot brushing his teeth before sex, both making an effort not to discuss the new member of the household, who at the moment was lying facedown on his pillow, trying not to see what he was seeing, the two of them crawling under the covers and turning off the light. Ozzie was barking somewhere in the yard, and some thoughts of Dad were trickling in now, quiet memories, like how he used to dust the roses for fungus every weekend, and the pegboard on the cellar wall with all his tools outlined in black, and the piles of *Home Craftsman* magazines under the stairs. Were they still there now, or had Elliot burned them? Then the harsher memories started creeping in, thoughts about his death, and I wiped those away by blinking my eyes. 30, 29, 28—I was counting myself down to sleep, the way I used to in prison. Finally I dropped off, despite Mimi's dog, whose name I couldn't recall. The last thing I remember, he or she was dozing at the foot of Elliot's bed.

4

The following day I reported to parole. Felix Ortega's office was in Tacoma, thirty minutes away. His corkboard was covered with pictures of his girlfriend, all taken outdoors, plus an EASY DOES IT sign and a ONE DAY AT A TIME. Entering my stats, he poked at the keys like he thought the computer might explode.

"Driver's license number?"

I didn't remember, I had to look in my wallet. He struggled with the keyboard for a while, but when I offered to help he gave me a chilly look.

"You know, I have to register you with the local police."

Ortega's white polo shirt was buttoned to the collar, he had tattoos down to his wrists, and at least four of his teeth were gold. "Why?" I said.

"The sex offender statutes. I guess you don't follow the news in prison."

My blood was starting to simmer. "That's all we did follow. Sir, I wasn't convicted of a sex offense."

"Well, I'm going to have to register you, anyway. And no calls to—" he checked the computer, "—Sandra Loyacano. No trips to Spokane."

"Why would I?" I said testily.

"Just so you know," he said.

I needed to stay on this guy's sunny side, Carl had made that very clear. So instead of getting in his face I drifted off, barely listening to my voice as he filled in the blanks on his screen.

"You know what jobs you can't hold," he said.

I nodded. "Anything requiring a license."

"Chauffeur, dry cleaner, funeral director—"

The bitter tone, the tattoos—I sat up as it dawned on me.

"—plumber, teacher, tree surgeon. You could try applying for federal bonding assistance, but with your sheet, I wouldn't count on it."

"Where did you do your time?" I asked, as casually as I could. I wasn't trying to piss him off, I thought maybe he'd relax if he knew I knew.

"You think you're pretty sharp, don't you, Hake?"

"No," I said. "Not at all."

"You oughta think about counseling people."

"Like sex offenders," I suggested. Get a grip, I thought.

"There's a real need in that area," he said.

I leaned toward him. "Except," I said, "I'd be leading a group of guys which I don't know what makes them tick."

Fortunately, he didn't take the bait. Whatever he had done, he was guilty of it, and he thought all cons who claimed otherwise were liars. He wasn't going to waste his time arguing. I sat back again.

"Now here's the deal," he said. "We have two contacts per month, plus one collateral contact. After six months, one per month and one collateral. Contacts to occur within three days of the first."

I said, "You didn't ask me my church affiliation."

"That's right, I didn't." He peered at the screen.

"And your therapist's name is Randy Nelson. Montlake Professional Building, Seattle. Supposed to be a good man."

"All right," I said.

"You didn't write it down," Ortega said.

"Could I have it again?" I said.

I looked up and he was on his feet. "This is *your* life, Hake," he said. "You're acting like it's somebody else's."

"Well," I said. "I did time for somebody else's crime. Maybe that accounts for it."

He glared at me. "Or maybe there's something you're afraid of finding out."

"For instance," I said.

"For instance, *why* you won't take responsibility. Why you're in denial about your crime. You ever been tested for attention disorder?"

Not while I was around, I thought, but let it go. When I sent Carl a postcard the next day, a view of Mt. Rainier, I told him my first parole meeting had gone okay, then added *P.S. Everybody looks like they're on work release,* something I had definitely noticed driving around the area, this grim, no-bullshit look, everybody on full alert, no eye contact, total jungle awareness, unless that was just me afraid to mix and mingle after so much down-time. Mimi certainly seemed to have the look, at least when I was around, and so did Ozzie the dog. Two weeks went by, she didn't say a word to me, no instructions about what work I was to do around the house, not from Mimi, not from Elliot—I was beginning to think she didn't trust me with the grocery money. I called Carl Williams's guy, Simon Lefcourt, but nobody called back. Then one day Mimi knocked on my door. "The moles have been at the lawn," she told me.

I went out and bought some strychnine pellets and some traps. Then, without being asked, I pruned the birch tree and turned all the planters, and then I walked the roof and pried up all the eaten-through shingles and replaced them. When I got to the rear of the house, I saw Mimi was watching me from the living room, drinking Bloody Marys from a pitcher, chewing on a celery stalk. Ozzie growled as I put away the ladder.

"Maybe I oughta take him for a walk," I suggested. "Get to know each other better."

She stroked the dog's head, blew out smoke. The ashtray on the patio table was full of butts. "April does that."

"April?"

She looked at me patiently. "The retarded girl? Lives down the street? The Hartigans' daughter. Wears a big Loden coat, walks all the neighborhood dogs—we talked about this."

"Right," I said. I must have been somewhere else at the time, but I didn't want to get into it with Mimi. I watched her pour herself another Bloody Mary.

"It's getting cold out here," she said, after a long gulp. "You want to go inside?"

"Sure," I said. It was my turn to be wary. While I built her a fire, she went into the kitchen. I could see her in there, fortifying her drink from the vodka bottle in the freezer. Then she was sitting in the chair behind me.

"I know what you're thinking," she said. "You think I'm still afraid of you and so far I've been noble and one minute I'm going to crack and order you out of here, but that's not going to happen."

I wasn't thinking any such thing. She got up to poke at the fire, and when she sat down again it was on the couch where I was sitting, and not far away, either. My stomach knotted up. She was Elliot's type not mine, skinny as a parking meter.

"It's not you. It's just not the best time in the world for Elliot and me. He's probably told you."

I wasn't sure what she meant. I said, "You're trying to have a baby."

"Something's holding him back," she said. "I think maybe he's worried about his genetics."

I eyed her. She was lighting a cigarette. "How so?"

She shook her head, amazed.

"You don't remember, he can't get it out of his head. The nightmares about the suicide, you don't have them?"

"No," I said.

Her head went back against the sofa pillow. "Elliot hasn't been in the cellar since we moved here. Which reminds me, the pilot light went out in the furnace."

"How long ago did the pilot light go out?" I wasn't as eager to talk about this as she was.

She chewed her ice. "At least he doesn't rail about it anymore," she said. Then she eyed me. "Are you uncomfortable talking about this?"

"What did he rail about?" I said.

"I'm sure you've heard it ten times over."

"Not necessarily," I said.

"The enemas? How he took the locks off your doors, so Elliot couldn't hide from the beatings?"

"No," I said. "I don't remember any enemas."

"And hypnotizing you? To make you stop masturbating?"

"No," I said. "Did he do that to Elliot? I know

he said he cured warts with hypnosis. Anyway, it's ancient history.''

"Well," she said, "if you want to hide your head in the sand."

I watched her leg swing slowly up and down. "You know," I said, "it wasn't ruled a suicide."

She looked at me carefully.

"Mom wouldn't have gotten the insurance. It had a suicide clause. He was cleaning the gun and it went off."

"Twice," said Mimi. "He shot himself twice. The first time he only creased his skull. I know Elliot told you all this."

"Yes, of course he did," I said.

She reached out and put her hand, the one without the cigarette, on my arm. "Elliot took a lot of shit for you, Denton."

"But you're right, I don't remember." It was Elliot who called the ambulance, I was too young and Mom was a basket case—in any event, I was seeing blood now, a curtain of it lowering behind my eyeballs. Mimi's hand was still on my arm, moving toward my hand.

I stood up suddenly.

She reared back as if I'd slapped her. The cold look came back into her face.

"By the way," she said, "those logs cost four dollars a fire. If you're going to build a fire every night, we'd better order a cord."

She ground out her cigarette and swept out of the room. Had she made some kind of pass? Whatever had happened, I tried to put it behind me, but her face floated up to me before I went to sleep, the sight of her chewing on the ice, working her tongue around her lips, sucking on the cigarette, leg moving up and down, and finally her hand sliding up my arm. I woke up in a cold sweat. The phone was ringing.

"Denton Hake?"

"Speaking," I said—that was what Dad always said when he didn't recognize the voice. I looked out the window and saw it was the next morning.

"This is Boris, I'm calling for Simon Lefcourt. Can you be here in two hours?"

So Carl's job lead panned out after all. The job site was out on Highway 99—I got lost on the way, arriving half an hour late at a bottle factory. Boris, the foreman, put me on cleanup, then switched me inside and showed me how they wanted the metal shelving assembled and bolted to the walls, which involved hauling 80-pound packages around without a handtruck. By the time I got home I was so whipped I fell right to sleep, using my tiredness as an excuse not to talk to Elliot or Mimi. I kept telling myself I'd misread her signals—hoping to God I'd misread them, for Elliot's sake.

Later that week I met Simon Lefcourt. I was playing poker at lunch—Boris told me he wanted to see me, in the trailer. Lefcourt was a big guy but compact like a little guy, small hands and a face full of worry creases. He asked me right off about my record.

"I never did what they said I did," I told him. I figured he wanted me to be direct.

"Try not to look back. The country's giving up on guys like you. How's Carl Williams doing?"

"Carl's hanging in there," I said.

"When they let Carl work, there's no one better."

Thank God for goodness, as my mom always said. To justify Lefcourt's trust I worked my ass off all week, I was like a poster child for rehabilitation, and even the old bitterness was draining away—I was thinking maybe Mom was right, I had passed God's test and this was my reward. All I had to do now was fulfill my counseling requirement, and I'd be home free. Friday night, when I got home from work, I looked for the number Ortega had given me— Randy something, I couldn't remember the last name, and the piece of paper wasn't in my wallet anymore. I looked through my pants, turned out the pockets.

That's when I found the three hundred dollars.

The bills were all crumpled up. Where had they come from? Not an ATM—there were fives and ones as well as twenties.

I started to hyperventilate. Think, I told myself, but all I could summon up was Sandra Loyacano— the lizard tattoo on her thigh. The breath left my body—the next thing I knew I was in the utility room staring at my other pair of pants.

I fell back against the pillow.

I lay there for a while, trying to clear my head, jumping here and there, from the utility room to my bedroom and back again. I heard a car door slam— Elliot and Mimi were back. It was their night to have dinner at a restaurant, then come back and make love, but they must have fought on the way back, because the bedroom door was closed and Elliot was in the kitchen.

"I heard you and Mimi had a little chat last week," he said when I came in.

My other pants were hanging over the dryer, but there was no therapist's name in the pocket. I started looking through my shirts.

"You told her you didn't remember two shots."

"What?" I said. I was barely listening. I kept thinking about Sandra Loyacano, the money they found on me the next day. Who did you rape this time, I thought—torturing myself, because I knew in my heart I hadn't done anything like that to anyone, and now that knowledge was degenerating into hope.

"It was in the coroner's report. Remember, I showed you?"

"Yeah, I remember," I said. I was picturing Dad, lying on the cellar floor, gun frozen in his hand, blood everywhere—it was like I was flashing on a Polaroid. I started refolding my shirts.

"No, you don't remember, I have to keep telling you. What are you looking for, why are you folding shirts?"

"Nothing. I thought I lost something, it's okay."

He glanced toward the bedroom and lowered his voice again. "I got my sperm count back, it's normal."

"Good," I said offhandedly. "That's good."

"Denton, can I ask you something?"

He had a pained look on his face. "Of course," I said.

"Is she drinking again?" he asked me.

I wanted to lie, he sounded so unhappy, but I knew I couldn't bring it off. "Mimi? Yeah, sometimes. Why," I said.

He let it sink in. "You can tell how much I love her, can't you?"

"Yes," I heard myself say.

"I've asked her to stop drinking. In case we're already pregnant."

"I see. Well, she hasn't."

"And the smoking."

I nodded. He had that priggish look that came over him sometimes.

"I hate to keep harping on it. It's like I don't have faith in her ability to control herself."

I thought of Mimi's hand on my hand. Suddenly, in the thick of my anxiety, I said something rash. "She's not running around on you, is she?"

He frowned at me. "Why do you ask that?"

I was all at sea. "You haven't screwed around on her," I said.

He looked at me like I'd asked him if he'd killed anybody. I took it back.

"I don't mean like Dad."

"Yeah, right," he said.

"I mean have you ever. Does she think you have. That's all I meant, Elliot, don't get upset—"

The doorbell was ringing. Right away Mimi yelled from the bedroom for Elliot to answer it. She sounded a little buzzed, but probably I was listening for that.

"Elliot," I said, following him to the front door, "*you're* the one who should forget about Dad. You're not like him, you're a saint compared to him—"

He bristled. "I don't compare myself to him," he said, "and no, Mimi and I have been totally faithful to each other." And he yanked open the door. On the other side was a person in a Loden coat, hood crimped forward like a monk's cowl.

"April, what is it? It's late."

It was a woman, and she was carrying a dog leash. She rubbed her thumb against her fingertips, indicating she wanted money. "Walkie walkies," she said. Ozzie rushed into the room, barking.

"I'm sorry," said Elliot to the woman, "I don't have cash right now."

"I do," I piped up, digging in my pocket. It was the retarded woman from down the street, April Har-⟶ tigan, the dog-walker—she was staring at me like she was trying to memorize my face. She could have been 18, she could have been 48—big sad eyes like a chimpanzee, jaw hanging open, and a nose that was twitching into some kind of sneer. Elliot took two twenties from my hand and gave them to her. She bent down and clipped the leash to Ozzie's collar, all the while keeping a wary eye on me. Elliot turned around—he looked suspicious too.

"Where'd you get all the cash?" he demanded.

Then it dawned on me. My heart suddenly relaxed.

"Simon Lefcourt pays in cash," I said.

"Does he?"

"What do you mean, does he? I just told you." I shoved the rest of the money back in my pocket. "It's Friday," I said. "Payday."

"You don't put it in the bank?"

"Elliot," I said—April the dog-walker was still eavesdropping, taking her sweet time adjusting Ozzie's leash. "It's not a problem. Why don't we stop worrying about each other. Mimi's calling you," I added, because she was—she was asking Elliot to bring her cigarettes. I closed the door on April Hartigan, headed back through the kitchen, through the yard and up to my room.

I locked the door.

I counted the money again. $320, that was about what I was earning a week. I started to hide it in Mom's gold-lettered Bible, the one she snaked from the Sands Hotel.

And that's when I saw my paycheck.

It was sitting right there on the night table.

I sat down on the bed, worked my thumbs into my temples.

It'll come back to me, I figured—the therapist's name. The truth is I was too scared to think.

5

It had an R in it, that's all I could remember. Finally I had to phone Felix Ortega—he was happy to yell at me for losing the number. I called it and got a receptionist. Dr. Nelson was in session, but my name was on a list. "When would you like to come in?"

"Whenever," I said. Suddenly I was sorry I had called. The receptionist put me on hold, then came back.

"How's two this afternoon?"

That was too soon. "Today? I'm working over in Tukwila."

"Then why don't we put you down for six."

So I had to agree to that—but all that morning, when I thought about having to tell a shrink about the $320 in my pocket, how did it get there, what that said about me and my criminal past, my tendency to drift off and see things I had no business seeing, my skin went cold and my mouth went dry.

They can't retry you, I kept telling myself. They paroled you, they can't send you back, no matter what you say to a shrink, it's privileged information.

Then I thought, who are you kidding, if they think you're going to commit violence, they're required by law to blow the whistle on you.

I went back and forth like this for hours, while trying to lose myself in the job. We were pouring concrete, the same crew as the day before, and I was working up a sweat, which helped take my mind off my confusions—but at the same time I felt like people were looking at me, either talking about me behind my back, or, when face to face, treating me with new respect. At lunch, playing cards, Boris and the others backed down every time I bluffed. When a white Cherokee with a busted taillight pulled up to the construction shed, next to Simon Lefcourt's brand-new black Cadillac, Boris gave me a friendly poke in the ribs and a there-you-go look I couldn't fathom at all.

"Was I right or wrong?"

A girl was getting out of the Cherokee, long legs, tight-sleeved T-shirt, little helmet of black hair with a streak of yellow in it.

"Tasty," I said, just to be polite. I couldn't make head or tail of his familiarity.

"I'll tell the boss you said so."

Simon Lefcourt had emerged from the shed—the girl was handing him something from her handbag, a present of some kind. Now he hugged her.

"*That's* Gwen," said Boris, like we'd discussed her in depth. My head began to hurt.

"Gwen?"

"Lefcourt's daughter."

I was losing it fast—I folded my hand.

"You're not quitting on us," said Boris.

I made an excuse. "I left the mixer running."

"Hake, sit down. Gimme a chance to win it back."

Win it back? I was only five bucks ahead.

Then it hit me. A chill went through me, like a breath of fresh air.

"How much did I win from you yesterday?"

Boris glanced around. "Anybody remember what that hand cost me?"

"Two hundred dollars," said one of the Chinese guys.

"Two hundred dollars," Boris repeated. "I don't think I want to play cards with you, Hake, if a hand like that is like an everyday occurrence."

"No, I remember it," I said. In fact it was coming back to me.

"Well, you played like you were someplace else."

"In the zone," the other Chinese guy suggested.

"It was four queens," I said.

"Four jacks," said Boris, "that's right, Mr. Poker Face."

"I remember," I said. I felt better and I felt worse. Suddenly I couldn't wait for quitting time. The girl—Gwen Lefcourt—was strolling past the game.

"Hi," she said.

She was saying it to the group, but she was looking at me.

"Hello," I said back. She gave me a smile and got into the beat-up Cherokee—Simon Lefcourt was waving at her from the shed, and she waved back, and the car went out the gate. I went back to the game and won a big hand—counted it carefully, fifty and change, put it in my pocket, and went back to work. My mind was bouncing like a pinball, first dreading the passage of time, then itching for the site manager to dismiss us, trying to decide what I was going to tell the doctor.

I got to Randy Nelson's office a little before six. It was a two-story building on the west side of Lake

Washington, nice neighborhood, shabby carpeting in the lobby, a dozen mail slots behind the desk, where the receptionist I'd spoken to was minding the phones and the fax machine. A few patients were waiting, a fat lady with a blotchy neck reading the Sierra Club News, a teenaged girl with ripped jeans and a baby in her arms. An important-looking guy came down the hallway to the desk, big head of gray hair—I perked up, expecting this to be Nelson, but he picked up his messages and went back upstairs, followed silently by the fat lady. Next, a woman in her thirties came down the stairs, dressed in jeans and a cashmere blazer—well-groomed and well-scrubbed and I was thinking, good, they take rich patients here too.

"Mr. Hake?"

It took me a moment to get it. She was pointing me up the stairs.

"I'm Randy Nelson," she said. "Second door on the right. What's it doing outside, is it raining yet?"

"Not yet," I said. I went on up. "That's Randi with an I?" I said—but then I saw the plaque on her door, RANDY NELSON, PhD.

"Why, did you expect a man?"

"I was told to," I said. "By my parole officer."

There were some huggy toys in one corner of her office, a Navajo blanket on one wall, but mostly the room was bare—one couch, two chairs. The window shades were down. On her desk was a computer and a tape recorder. I took the chair nearest the door, she sat down on the couch. "I was named for my grandmother," she said.

I felt awkward as could be. "Names are important."

"Yes, they can be."

I heard myself start to babble. "Homers and Egberts don't do well in school—I read that once. And I never met a Joy I didn't like." What a dork, but she smiled at me, the kind of smile I like, no teeth, just lips. And her body looked limber, not that I was studying it.

"I wouldn't think there'd be many Egberts left."

"No, probably not," I said. Her hair was older than her face, iron gray but with a dyed look, and her eyes were large and dark.

"So what's a Denton?" she said. She said it pleasantly, but I stiffened up.

"A guy who's gotta be here, I guess."

That wouldn't do—I could tell from the hard look she gave me.

"A Denton," I said, "is an innocent man."

This seemed to take her by surprise—she was quiet for a moment. I noticed a small hickey on her neck, right above the collarbone, and the ghost of a wedding ring on her third finger. I was trying to stay focused.

"How old are you, Mr. Hake?"

"Denton is good. I'm thirty-four."

"Married?"

"No," I said. "Are you?"

She didn't bat an eye. "I used to be. Are you currently employed?"

"Yes, ma'am. I'm working construction—the Lefcourt Company. I'm living in Auburn with my brother and his wife."

She was writing it all down—I was wishing she wouldn't, but then I didn't want to be tape-recorded, so I didn't object.

"And your parents?"

"My mom lives by herself. In the house we grew up in."

"And your dad?"

Rain started to patter at the windows. "My dad died when I was a kid."

"That must have been rough."

I listened to the rain. I was out there in it, I could almost feel it on my face. I was struggling to stay put.

"—did he die?"

I blinked. "Yes. I just told you."

"What did he die of, Mr. Hake?"

The chair was eating at my tailbone. I shifted around in my seat. "Gunshot wound," I said.

It was her turn to blink. "How did that happen?"

"Two gunshot wounds. First he just shot the side of his face off." I remembered Elliot putting it that way. Randy Nelson winced.

"How awful," she said.

"That's why I'm such a pessimist," I said. Wind blew a sheet of rain across the windows. "Somebody told me that once." I started to say Carl Williams, but I stopped myself.

"What were the circumstances?"

I was trying to cooperate, picture Dad dead, but I couldn't. "I was at home. I don't know. They say I heard the shot and found the body, but all I remember is what I've been told."

"You were how old?"

"Ten or twelve. My brother Elliot was in his first year of high school. Yeah, so I was ten. It was ruled accidental, but that was for the insurance."

She wrote that down.

"Are you taking any medication?"

"None. Not even vitamins."

"Have you ever been in therapy before?"

"Not counting my caseworker? No. You mean after Dad died? No, my mom took us to see the minister."

"Any history of head trauma?"

I watched the windows, trying to stay this side of them. "Why, do I seem that way to you?"

"The state makes us follow this protocol. Are you a high-school graduate?"

"Yes," I said. And then I admitted, "Just barely. I was bad at taking tests." The rain was loud in my ears. "My dad used to call me a Dull Normal."

A muscle twitched in her cheek. "To your face?"

"That's an IQ term."

"Yes, I know," she said.

I was looking in my lap. "He was being sarcastic. He thought I was smart, he just thought I behaved like a retard."

She got up to close the window—the wind was starting to blow the rain in. She didn't say a word, just cocked her head at me, and before I could stop myself the words popped out.

"I tend to forget things," I said.

She took that in stride. She must know that already, I thought.

"Like what things?" she asked.

I grinned at her. "I forget."

She looked at me patiently. I took a deep breath. Nothing came out. Then I heard myself talking.

"I won some money at poker yesterday," I said, "and when I found it in my pocket, I didn't realize where it had come from."

She nodded, like this was exactly what she expected to hear. That really unsettled me.

"Did you think you had stolen it?"

For a second I considered lying, but I didn't. "Yes," I said.

"Has this happened to you before?"

Careful, I thought—I was picturing Sandra Loyacano. She was in the changing room at the sporting-goods store and I was handing clothes in to her. "I used to space out a lot in prison," I said.

"Most people do. And before prison?"

Her eyes were bright, my guard was down. "I have this tendency to drift off," I said.

"In what sense?"

Stop now, I thought, but I couldn't. "I kind of leave my body," I said.

I waited for her to say something, but she didn't so much as blink.

"That's what it feels like," I said.

"And when did this begin?"

"My mom called it daydreaming. To me it's like I'm really there. This friend of mine in prison, he always knew when it was happening." I looked down at the floor.

"Denton? What just went through your mind?"

Something must have showed in my face—I was still thinking about Sandra Loyacano, the lizard tattoo on her thigh.

"My mom says I used to steal things out of her drawers."

"How old were you?"

"I don't know. Eleven or twelve. After Dad died. And from stores."

She started to write this down—then put her pen aside. "You don't remember doing that?"

"Sometimes. Mom kept saying we were poor now. Maybe I thought I was helping out. She never made me give the stuff back."

"And you think that might have contributed?"

"To what?"

"To your landing in prison."

I felt myself start to shut down.

"It didn't turn me into a rapist."

She frowned at me. "A rapist?"

"You may be right about the stealing. Yes, I gave Mom the money. She told me they were going to repossess her car, and she didn't want to ask my brother for any more. Anything else in my file is a lie."

She shook her head. "I wasn't referring to your file."

"But it's there, isn't it. What they charged me with originally. It's all bullshit," I said, sitting forward in the chair. "I don't care what I can or can't remember, if you put a gun to my head I couldn't rape a woman. As far as stealing, okay, maybe I was in her house, supposedly I saw her naked, because I knew about the tattoo on her leg, but she tried on clothes in the store, that's when I saw the tattoo."

She nodded—I was looking her straight in the eye. "Why do you think you couldn't rape a woman?"

"You don't believe me. Fine. Look, this has been very illuminating." I started to get up.

"We still have a few minutes. I believe you, Denton, but I think it's important that you tell me why."

"Honest to God? I don't think I could sustain an erection," I said, "if I thought the woman was in pain. Now you probably think I'm kissing your ass."

"No," she said, "I don't," and she started to get up from her chair—I felt like I had won some tiny victory. "Next time I'd like to give you some tests."

"Next time?" I said. Red color was swimming in my head.

"They have you down for two sessions a week. How's a week from Friday for you? And then Tuesdays and Fridays after that."

"I don't know," I said. I was edging toward the door. "I only make three hundred a week."

"It's ten dollars a session," said Randy Nelson. "And the State makes up the difference."

Yes, I thought, and then they nail you to the cross. "That's good to know," I mumbled.

"So Friday the seventh then?"

"Yeah, fine," I said, just to get out of there. I was afraid if I hung around any longer, she'd remember to ask me my phone number. I thanked her and said goodbye, walked back down the stairs and out to the parking lot. By my watch it was seven o'clock—had I really been there an hour?

Don't get sucked in, I thought. She's not on your side, she's a government employee—if it wasn't for the government, you wouldn't have to talk to her in the first place, much less two times a week. You'll end up dreading every Tuesday and Friday, the way you used to dread Friday nights, Dad's night to be with Dot, therefore Mom's night to sob in her room and throw shoes against the wall. Maybe I won't go back at all, I was thinking.

Mom's car was outside Elliot's house when I got home. I needed to lie down, I needed a nap, but halfway up the driveway I heard Mimi call my name.

"I'll be right in," I told her. She was in a harsh mood.

"You ate all the salmon dip," she told me. "I asked you not to. Never mind, your mom's here."

I followed her inside. Elliot was making small talk with Mom, all lovey-dovey with Mimi on the couch for Mom's benefit. I sat there thinking about Randy

Nelson, all the crap she'd want to hear about my dad, how I should hate him more than I did.

"How's the job?" Mom asked me.

"The job? It's good."

"Learning anything?" said Elliot.

"Sure," I said. "I'm learning how good a poker player I am."

"I think we can find you a better job," said Elliot.

"It's an okay job," I insisted. I was eyeing Mom, thinking how I'd been discussing her this afternoon— and watching Elliot and Mimi, too, thinking how much sweeter Mimi must have been before I came into their lives, or Elliot would never have bothered going near her. "This Lefcourt's a good guy," I said.

"Why, because he hires ex-cons?" said Elliot. The front doorbell was ringing—he disengaged from Mimi. "There's more than meets the eye there," he said, and opened the door. Outside was April Hartigan, the retarded girl, come to take Ozzie for his walk—I saw her peer around the jamb at me. Ozzie came padding into the hall.

"She's been gossiping about you," Mimi said to me, after Elliot closed the door on April.

"Who has?" I looked toward the street—April was making Ozzie heel. "You mean the dog-walker."

"Mrs. Fabricant up the street—April walks Selma, her golden retriever? She asked me how long you'd spent in prison."

"It's none of their business," said Mom.

"That's right, it isn't," said Elliot, sitting down again.

I drained my drink. "Well, I'll be out of your hair soon," I said.

They all looked at me. "What are you talking

about?'' said Elliot. ''Don't get paranoid.''

''I know what I know,'' I said. ''And I know I'm better off on my own. As soon as I get two months' rent in the bank, I'm out of here.''

That was all Mimi needed to hear. ''If that's what he really wants,'' she said with a look at Elliot.

''No,'' said Elliot, and shot a we-talked-about-this look back at her. ''We want you here. We like having you around. End of conversation.''

And it was. Mom left right after dinner, and I went straight up to my room. I watched TV for a while, then crawled into bed and opened the Gideon to a favorite passage. *The race is not to the swift, nor the battle to the strong, neither yet bread to the wise, nor yet riches to men of understanding,* and so forth. Life isn't fair—these verses soothed me, as they often had in prison. That started me thinking about church, how I'd promised the parole board I'd join one, though officially I wasn't obliged to, and about Dad dropping the three of us off at University Bible Church so he could get in a Sunday morning quickie with Dot, all jumbled together with thoughts about Sandra Loyacano. Yes, her address was on the check. No, I couldn't remember the inside of her house, but I knew her mom drove a two-seater Mercedes, so I must have seen it, or did Sandra just tell me about it? I tried to picture the car, but all I kept seeing was a white Cherokee, Gwen Lefcourt at the wheel. Let it go, I thought, stop beating up on yourself, and I dropped off to sleep—pretty soon I was back in a cell, pissing in a chrome toilet. I woke up and I had to urinate—I lay there, thinking about Randy Nelson and everything I'd blabbed to her. Moron, I thought, now they're gonna lock you on a mental ward. Finally I got up and relieved myself, then read Ecclesiastes some more, until I calmed down enough to turn off the light. Elliot and Mimi were arguing in the bedroom, or rather Mimi was complaining about me and Elliot was trying to placate her, all right in front of my eyes—Mimi's language got coarser and crazier, until I couldn't hear her anymore. Gwen Lefcourt tiptoed in and out of my thoughts again, and I fell into a dreamless sleep.

6

Later that week, the site manager called me over in the middle of the morning, gave me a purchase order for some lumber and acoustic tile, and told me to deliver it to a store called Fay's Big & Tall.

The store was part of a mini-mall in Renton. I was a little out of my depth with the repair work, but by late afternoon I had it ready to plaster. Traffic in the store was light—the two salesgirls, one blonde, one Eskimo, neither one tall, neither one fat, spent most of their time rearranging the jewelry displays, reading the travel magazines on the coffee table, and trying to agree on a radio station.

Gwen Lefcourt came in about five o'clock. She took a quick look through the register, opened up the jewelry cases, moved some brooches around, then came over to inspect my work.

"Hi," she said, before I did. "This looks great," she said.

I said, "Another day should do it." She asked me if I could match the paint—the old cans had been thrown out—and I told her not to worry. "I saw you the other day," I said.

When she turned around she was smiling. "Where?"

"At the job site. What was it, your dad's birthday?"

"That's right," she said. "You were playing poker." She frowned, then nodded. "Well, I'm glad he sent me somebody good."

"Denton," I said, putting out my hand.

"Gwen."

She was wearing a silk blouse, no visible bra, and her lipstick was pink. "It's a real attractive store," I said.

"Thank you," she said. "Tell a friend," she added, with a quick little smile.

"Who's Fay?" I asked.

She opened the changing room door—hanging there was a picture of a plump rosy-cheeked lady in a flowery hat. It was a famous painting, I knew that much. "That's Fay," she said.

"The fat girl inside you struggling to get out."

She eyed me—we were studying each other. I noticed a mole on her cheek, too close to her mouth to be called a beauty mark. Her eyes were brown with sparks of gold, dark and light, like her yellow-streaked black hair. "I hope not," she said. "I don't trust fat people."

"Uh-huh," I said. "So why—"

"Large sizes are growing, small sizes aren't."

"That's interesting," I said.

"That's how I convinced Simon. My dad."

"To invest?" She nodded, and I glanced around at the empty store, the two tiny, skinny salesgirls. "What about hiring a tall person?" I suggested.

She met my gaze. "I bet *you* could sell clothes to women."

For a paranoid second, I thought she was alluding

to Sandra Loyacano. "You know, I bet I could," I said, recovering.

"Would you like some coffee?"

There was a cappuccino machine in the corner, plus a tray of doughnuts. She took a bite of one, slowly wiped her lips, and sat beside me—our legs touched, I felt the pressure, and the next thing I knew, I had my first public hard-on since getting out of prison. That's how much, I realized, I'd been holding myself in check.

"You know what the average American woman weighs? Five foot four, hundred forty pounds."

"You're kidding," I said.

"One in three ladies is big. More size eighteens than eights." She gazed sadly around the store, then called to one of the salesgirls. "Bettina, when you get those receipts done you can leave." To me, she said, "This is not a typical day."

"I was wondering," I said politely.

"Usually it's even slower. My dad is so disappointed."

"I bet he isn't."

"You're sweet," she said, squeezing my arm, and bounded up again at the sound of the chimes.

A guy was coming in the door. At that same moment I noticed the ring on her left hand—a diamond.

"Richard, hi," she said. She gave him a peck on the cheek, they exchanged some words I couldn't hear, and then to my surprise she brought him over to me. He had a ponytail, leather jacket, close-together eyes behind wire-frame glasses. "Richard Nesbit, this is Denton—"

"Hake," I said, wiping my hand on my trousers. He left it dangling in midair.

"Denton thinks I should hire a fat lady."

"A tall lady," I corrected. I put my hand away.

"Richard helped design this mini-mall."

"Is that so," I said.

"He's working with my dad now. They're bidding on a project together."

He cut this short. "Gwen, we're late," he said.

"Good luck," I said—the guy Richard still hadn't made eye contact, and I felt like busting him in the mouth. He rapped on the new wall a couple of times, then led Gwen out to his gold Lexus, hand on her ass—but as Gwen got into the car, she glanced back through the door, wiggled her fingers at me, and gave me a long wink.

That was all it took, that and the silk blouse she was wearing. All the way home I heard her voice in my ear, telling me I was sweet. I didn't jerk off to her, though—I wanted the feeling to last.

As for Richard Nesbit, I erased him from my mind.

The next day, Saturday, Gwen wasn't there—according to the Eskimo salesgirl, Bettina, she was making the rounds of the swap meets. I tried to figure out some way to make the job last more than two days, but the site manager wanted me back on Monday.

And then Monday morning she showed up at the site again. Her dad was there, and they had a conversation in the shed that lasted over an hour. I was supposed to be laying tile, but I kept ducking out to make sure I didn't miss her departure. When I saw her leave the shed, I walked over to where her Cherokee was parked.

"Oh, I'm glad you found me," she said—big smile. "I forgot to pay you the other day."

"But I'm working for your dad."

"No, you did such a good job."

That made me feel bold. "You know how you can pay me?" I said. "Let me buy you lunch."

She smiled brightly. "Okay." My heart leaped up, but then sank again—beyond, in the parking lot, I saw Felix Ortega, my parole officer, getting out of a gray Dodge. He'd seen me, too—nowhere to hide.

I excused myself to Gwen, ambled over, not too fast.

"You on a break?" said Ortega. He was carrying a briefcase.

"I was about to go to lunch," I said. I glanced back at Gwen, hoping Ortega would get the message and take pity on me. She was watching. "I just made plans."

"Well, it'll only take a minute." He sat himself down on a shelving carton, opened up his briefcase. I caught a glimpse of a gun holstered inside—a .45. "You missed an appointment," he said.

"I didn't. What day is today?"

"Fifth day of the month."

"I'm sorry. Jesus," I said, looking back at Gwen again—now Simon Lefcourt was watching from the doorway to the shed. To Ortega I said, "Hey, I went to see Randy Nelson. The therapist you said was a good man. Not true."

Ortega looked at me sharply. "That's not for you to judge."

"It was a girl, not a guy."

"So," he said.

"So," I said, "you were wrong."

"Why are you getting hot with me?" he said.

"I'm not getting hot with you."

"Yes, you are. You're trying to pick a fight."

"Have it your way," I said. "Does the State of Washington issue you that gun?"

"No," he said.

"What good does it do you in your briefcase?"

He handed me a paper to sign, then snapped the briefcase shut. "I don't like what I'm seeing here. First a missed appointment, now all this attitude."

Attitude? Parole officer's dream, was how I saw myself. I eased next to him on the carton, one eye on Gwen. Simon had gone back into the shed, and she was still looking my way—I was praying she hadn't heard anything. "I'll tell you what's eating me," I said, lowering my voice. "You did what you did, I didn't. You're the one with the criminal conscience, and I've got to account to you for everything I do."

He blinked at me. "I'll expect you two weeks from tomorrow."

That was that. I waited till he was back in his Dodge, then doubled back to Gwen. Her car keys were out. "Friend of yours?" she asked.

"Not exactly," I said. I got into her Cherokee.

"I know where let's go," she said—she tapped my knee and threw the car into gear. We drove to a burger place on the lake, talked about the clothing business on the way, how much money she owed her dad—not the amount, just how much it was weighing on her.

"Business'll pick up," I said. "If it's as good a business as you say."

The temperature was in the fifties, warm enough to sit out on the deck. Gwen was watching the water, squinting her eyes to catch the sunlight. "I think I'm just perverse."

"Why? Because you don't like fat ladies and you opened up a store?"

She laughed at that.

"I guess we're both looking for a life," I said. As soon as I said it, I wished I could take it back—there was a look in her eyes that told me she knew more than I wanted her to. Toward the end of the meal, while I was picking at her fries, she came out with it.

"How did you stand it?" she said.

"Stand what?"

"Prison." She said it quietly. "That guy was your parole agent, wasn't he?"

"Yes," I said. To my relief, I saw a look of kindness in her eyes. "I guess your dad clued you in?"

She shrugged. "You're not the first ex-convict he's hired."

"I know that," I said.

"Used to drive my mom crazy. Drove her out of the house—that and a million other issues."

"Sounds like Mimi."

She frowned. "Mimi?"

"My sister-in-law. I'm living with my brother, she's not too thrilled about it. Thank God for people like your dad."

I didn't mean to sound so holy, but that's how it came out. "Yes, thank God," she said, looking in her bag. The waitress was putting the check down—before I could reach for my wallet, Gwen had her Visa out.

"What were you in for?" she asked.

"Burglary," I said. Was she testing me, had her dad told her everything? "And assault," I heard myself say.

She frowned. "You don't strike me as the type."

"I'm not," I assured her. I was tempted to explain about my guilty plea, just in case, then decided against it. Next I'd be airing all my doubts and worries. Instead, I said, "So you must know Carl Williams."

Now she looked away. "Who?" she said.

"He gave me your father's name? Black guy?"

"Carl Williams," she repeated. "Sounds familiar." The waitress was back—Gwen looked grateful for the interruption.

"Do you have another card?" said the waitress. "This one redlined."

Gwen opened her bag in her lap. "I think I left them all home," she said, throwing me an apologetic look—no need, my wallet was already out. I was going to press her about Carl, but on the way out to her car she hooked her arm through mine.

"So what are you doing Friday night?" she asked.

I told her I had nothing planned. She took a pen from her address book and wrote an address on my palm.

"Anytime after eight," she said.

"What about that guy Richard?" I said.

"What about him?" she said brightly.

I liked the sound of that and I didn't.

"Hey, I'm just asking you to a party," she said. "There'll be a lot of people there, I'll be one of them."

"And Richard too," I said.

"It's his house," she said. "Do you care?"

I did care, but I kept it to myself. We drove back to the job site, quiet now, smiling at each other every few blocks, and it was the smile I recalled, plus the feel of her pen on my palm, and the anxious look in her eyes when she talked about disappointing her dad. All afternoon I worked like a fiend, hardly working up a sweat, and her face kept floating up to me at dinner, though that was sad in a way—in the old days, if I met a girl I liked, I'd always tell Elliot, and vice versa, but that night I didn't, if only because Mimi now seemed to be giving him the silent treatment and he might not take much pleasure in my news. Unmentioned, Gwen stayed in my mind—she was the first thing I brought up when I sat down again in Randy Nelson's office.

"I'm feeling better," I said, in answer to her first question, and tried to smile. With my parole officer following me around, I figured I should try to stay on my therapist's good side. "Actually, I met a girl."

Randy sat there with her hands clasped behind her neck, listening. I was going to tell her how Gwen Lefcourt was seeing this other guy, Richard, but she didn't seem as interested in Gwen as I was. Her computer was on, and she asked me to sit at the desk.

"This is that test I talked to you about," she said. She had it all booted up, I was supposed to take it right then and there.

"You know how to use a mouse?"

"Couldn't this be take-home?" I asked lightly.

"I'm afraid not." She watched me sit down. "Just click off the box that applies, no time pressure."

Gee, thanks, I thought—I was definitely not in the mood, but what choice did I have? I scrolled down the list of questions.

Some people have the experience of driving or riding in a car or bus or subway and suddenly realizing that they don't remember what has happened during all or part of the trip. Click a

box to show what percentage of the time this
happens to you.

0% 10 20 30 40 50 60 70 80 90 100%
(*never*)   (*always*)

Some people find that sometimes they are listening to someone talk and they suddenly realize that they did not hear part or all of what was
said. Click a box to show what percentage of the
time this happens to you—

And so forth, for 28 questions in all. *Do you talk
to yourself? Does life ever seem like a dream? Do
you hallucinate? Do you feel like two different people? Are you out of your goddamn mind?*
It all seemed pretty dumb to me, but I played
along, clicking off numbers. 10. 20. 30. 20. 10. 20.
30. *Some people find evidence they have done things
they don't remember doing.* Yeah, but don't tell the
government. *Some people get accused of lying. Some
people can ignore pain. Some people hear voices.
Some people feel they're in two places at once. Some
people are duck-fucking crazy.*
I finished and went back to the other chair. "I
suppose this all goes into my file."
Randy was looking at the screen. "You skipped a
couple of questions," she said.
"No," I said. "Which?"
She showed me.

Some people have the experience of feeling
they are watching themselves do something and
they actually see themselves as if they were
looking at another person. Click a box—

"Does that ever happen to you?" Randy asked.

"Can I plead the Fifth?" I said, as pleasantly as I could. And the moment I said it, I saw us both, me in the chair, Randy at her computer, swiveling back toward me.

"And this one—you said sometimes you feel like you leave your body—"

"What's the purpose of this test? Who else is gonna see it now?"

"No one but you and me," she said.

"You, me, and the computer."

"You want to tell me why you're so suspicious?"

"Because you're giving me tests," I said, listening to my voice—angry and hoarse. "Don't tests piss you off?"

"Not as a rule," said Randy, picking lint off her sleeve. She had on an all-black outfit today, sweater and slacks. "So what about this girl you met?" she asked.

"There's nothing to tell," I said. "We had lunch together." I watched her drum her fingers on her chair. "What does your husband do for a living?"

"My husband?"

"Your ex-husband."

"Video artist. How does Wendy feel about your prison record?"

"Gwen," I said, and I nodded toward the computer. " '*Some people forget what people have just said to them.*' "

She ignored that. "Does she know you've spent time in prison?"

"Yes, she knows. Her father hires ex-cons, she's used to it. She's a nice person." Then I blurted something. "She's got a boyfriend."

"I see."

"I think she's phasing him out."

"For you."

"I didn't say that," I said. For some reason I was picturing Mom—down in the basement doing laundry, not ten feet away from Dad's workbench, which was exactly as he'd left it the night he put a bullet in his face and then a bullet in his head. It was there before my eyes and then it wasn't.

"Denton? What just went through your mind?"

I shook my head. "Nothing. My mom."

"What about your mom?"

I could see her pouring in the detergent, Dad's tools hanging on the wall, the cartons of magazines, the drawer where he kept his revolver.

"I know what you're getting at," I said.

"What?" said Randy.

"You think there's something big I'm trying to forget," I said. "And that makes me forget the little things."

"And what do you think?"

I looked at her. "It's plausible," I said, thinking what if this is true, what if my brain's as full of holes as an ant farm, what else didn't I remember, like maybe getting fucked up the ass in prison? I said, "I remember what happened afterwards."

"After you found your dad's body?"

"After I called Elliot."

"What's the first thing you remember?" she said.

I couldn't call it up. All I could picture was Mom turning on the washing machine. I could almost hear it hum.

"Part of my dad's skull was blown off. Elliot made me fit it back on and hold it, while he called the ambulance."

That made her blink. For a couple of seconds she didn't say anything.

"You were ten years old?"

"Yes."

"And you remember that."

"Yes. Or Elliot told me. I don't know." I looked at the floor. "You think that's why my mind drifts away?" I said. "Because I saw something horrible?"

Randy gave a little shrug. "Or because you didn't see it."

"And that got to be a habit."

She nodded. "The question is, what does your body do while your mind's not paying attention?"

I squirmed in the chair. Fool, I thought, now she's certain you raped Sandra Loyacano. As you sit here, she's building her case. "I think the hour's up," I said, pretending to glance at my watch.

It wasn't, but she let it go. "So on Friday," she said, "maybe you could come a little earlier."

"All right," I said. I didn't think I was late, but I didn't press that point, either. As soon as I hit the street I forgot about the test, but now Dad's face kept swimming up to me. I was thinking about that last afternoon, me and Elliot tossing a ball around, Dad deadheading the roses, the phone ringing every fifteen minutes, then hanging up when Mom answered. Now Gwen Lefcourt's face suddenly drifted up again, licking powdered sugar off her lips—suddenly I was hungry, suddenly I remembered Mimi had given me a shopping list. The party was called for ten—I bought groceries, drove home, had dinner with Elliot and Mimi, who for some reason weren't dining out on their lovemaking night.

"We've got good news," Elliot said, over coffee.

"We've decided to adopt," said Mimi.

They both put on smiles. One of them didn't want this, I couldn't figure out who.

"But you'll still be having sex," I said.

They laughed politely. I guessed it was Elliot who didn't want to adopt—that meant Mimi wanted to go on drinking.

"Listen," I said to him later—we were out back, pitching horseshoes, "the day you sign adoption papers, she'll probably conceive."

He had something else on his mind. "How are the sessions going?"

I was taken aback. This was the first time he had asked about my therapy. "They're going okay."

"You ever talk about Dad?"

"No, not too much," I said.

I sounded guarded, and we both heard it. "But you do talk about him," he said.

"His death," I said. "I've been thinking about his death."

"What about it?"

"I don't know. Trying to remember. She wants me to remember."

"Don't let her talk you into anything."

"Yeah, I know," I said. I had an hour drive to the party, it was time to think of getting dressed.

"You know what I've always thought?" he said. "I thought he killed himself to keep himself from killing her. It was his one unselfish act."

I put my hand on his shoulder. "You know, I think Randy might have an hour free."

He managed to laugh at this. "What's the worst thing he ever did to you?" I said.

He frowned. "Did your shrink tell you to ask that?"

"*I'm* asking," I said.

He thought it over. "In terms of lifelong impact? I guess letting me watch him have sex with Dot."

I frowned. "Letting you," I said.

"In the sense of not closing the door," said Elliot. "In the sense of not caring if I was home to see it. Of course, Dot was a whore. She went along with it, she encouraged it."

"And that was worse than the spankings?"

"Spankings," he said, with a hollow laugh. "Is that how you remember them?"

"I *don't* remember," I said. I was watching a pigeon waddle across the horseshoe pit.

"Taking the lock off my door, so I couldn't hide?"

"Yes, Mimi mentioned that—"

"And those inhalers? In his night table? Little pieces of snot clinging to the ends? He used to snort them like cocaine."

"I never saw those," I said. The pigeon flapped onto a pine branch.

"Oh, yes you did. I caught you sniffing one once, I almost beat the shit out of you. And those pills he used to bring home for Mom. Mood elevators. First he cheated on her, then he drugged her."

"Okay," I said. I didn't care to hear him rant any more—we finished the game and he went back inside. Later, dressing with the window open, I heard Elliot and Mimi jawing at each other—from what I could gather, she was pissed off at him for telling me about their adoption plans. I left for the party without saying goodbye.

Richard Nesbit's house was more than an hour's drive, in a gated community called Oaktree Estates. His gold Lexus was in the garage, but it was his parents' house—they were off in Costa Rica or someplace. A working architect, and he was still partying at Mom and Dad's—well, who was I to talk. Out back were two acres, a couple of nice oak trees with a dance floor set up between, a DJ, tables with heaters, silver chafing dishes. I walked around looking for Gwen. Richard Nesbit was there, his ponytail done up in a turquoise ring, all puffed up about something—waving his arms around like a TV preacher, spellbinding two high-school-looking girls who were trailing around after him. One time I tried to catch his eye, but he looked right past me. Then, "Boo," I heard behind me—it was Gwen.

"Glad you could make it," she said. I'd been thinking how bold it was for her to have me there, at her boyfriend's house, but now here was Richard with the high-school girls.

"Did you say hello to our host?" she said.

"No, did you want me to?"

She laughed at that, asked me to wait while she chatted with some people—a lot of the guests were her invitees, sorority sisters, people in the clothing business, some fat ladies I thought might be customers, plus a guy who looked enough like Travis Tritt to be Travis Tritt. She was gone awhile—I got myself a beer and made my way over to Richard Nesbit. He was holding forth on something or other—I waited till the people he was talking to got bored, then sidled past him.

"Nice party, Dick. Great house."

"No," he said.

"I'm sorry, I **thought** you lived here."

"The name is **Richard**." He didn't crack a smile. "Enjoy," he said, moving away before I could say my name or remind him where we'd met. I watched him go into a bathroom, closing the door after him, then walked back to where Gwen was talking, by the bar. Five minutes before I'd been invisible, now I was getting stares, from a couple of ladies who'd seen me talking to Gwen.

"I said hello to your boyfriend. Richard Don't Call Me Dick."

"Richard's a little testy tonight," Gwen said. I glanced around and saw Richard come out of the bathroom, then duck back inside again. Beyond, one of the high-school-looking girls bolted up from a coke mirror, barking at him to close the door. So that's how it is, I thought.

"Dance?" I said to Gwen.

She was watching the bathroom, too. There was nobody on the dance floor.

"Come on, we'll break the ice."

The song was Emmylou Harris, quiet enough to slow-dance to. I got a hard-on and she pretended not to notice. When we came off the floor, she sat down at Richard's table, back-to-back with him. He was talking to the girl from the bathroom, pretending to ignore us.

"How was your week?" I said to Gwen.

"It sucked," she said. "I'm into penalty on my mortgage."

I refilled our glasses from the wine bottle on the table. "Can't your dad help out?"

She shrugged. "He's really starting to think I'm a flake."

"And you want to prove yourself."

She nodded, gulping at her wine. "Sometimes I wish I had a brother."

"Take the pressure off," I said.

"Exactly."

Richard was eavesdropping now. "Your dad expects a lot," I said.

"Does he ever. This is bumming me out, do you want a real drink?"

"I'm fine," I said. Across the lawn, some blitzed-out guy was trying to climb one of the oak trees, while a guy with a stopwatch timed him and three girls in Spandex and silk pelted him with clumps of dirt. "What this party needs is more assholes," I said. Gwen laughed, and laid her cheek briefly on Richard's shoulder—he was turned round in his chair now, gray eyes like smoky flags, way pinned. He got up from the table, without a word—the high-school girl pitty-patted after him. I took Gwen's hand.

"Another dance?"

She shook her head. We walked toward the oak tree—I had half a mind to climb it, because I was sure I could beat the last guy's time. I pulled her close, gave her a kiss for anyone to see. She put her tongue in my mouth—I felt the ground give way and a moment later we were lying by the pool, far enough from the lights and the heaters so the stars were visible in the sky. A second contestant was starting up the tree. I kissed her again, longer this time. I could picture us locked there on the pool deck—no, it was Richard Nesbit I was seeing, in his bedroom, his hand down the back of the high-school girl's cutoffs. I opened my eyes.

"What about your fiancé?" I said.

"He's not," she said, and gazed idly around.

"He didn't give you that ring?"

She shrugged. "Obviously," she said, "we're starting to see other people." She stretched out on her back—I stayed propped on one elbow, watching the climbers. "So beautiful," she said. She was talking about the stars.

"Yeah, but nothing like we look from a plane," I said. I lay down beside her. "You ever notice that?"

She frowned. "Notice what?"

"That's why there's so much evil in the world," I said. "That's my mom's theory."

"What theory." She was tensing up her face like she was fighting off dizziness.

"God's jealous of His creation, he's angry at mankind, because a city at night looks more impressive from the air than the night sky looks from the ground."

Her eyes were swimming. "Your mom said that or you said that?"

"My mom," I said. I was so full of lust, she didn't even look beautiful to me anymore.

"Is your mom very religious?"

"Very," I said. I kissed her again. Somebody trotted past the pool and called something to Gwen I didn't catch—she sat up, and I saw Richard running toward us across the patio.

"We need to talk," he said. He grabbed Gwen's wrist and yanked her to her feet.

"Hey, take it easy," I said.

"Fuck off, jerk."

That tore it. In two seconds he was up against the pool-shed and my hand was around his throat. I could see us there, the two of us, me about to smash his head against the wall, but I stopped myself. I backed away, or thought I did—no, he was lying on the ground, clutching his face, and two of the tree-climbers were trying to hustle me across the lawn. I shook them off, slammed one of them up against the house and headed for the front gate, where Gwen was waiting. Richard was loping after me, so slowly I knew he didn't want to catch up just now, still holding his jaw where I'd clocked him. Blood was streaming from his nose.

"I'll sue your ass," he cried. I blasted through the gate. Gwen whirled. I half expected her to tell me to get lost. There I was, trying to ease back into myself, get control.

"Would you follow me home please?"

Her car door slammed and I trotted toward my Nova, glancing back at Richard—he was peering through his gate now, gripping the bars like the back lawn was a prison yard. "You fucking whore!" he was screaming. "I'll fucking kill you!" I got into my car—his fraternity brothers, if that's what they were, started dragging him away from the fence.

I followed Gwen home. She drove over 50 all the way—we passed the mini-mall where her store was and then I lost track of where we were. She pulled to the curb—for a second I thought she was lost, too, because the neighborhood was fairly ratty, not even half-gentrified, but when I pulled to the curb she went on ahead into a gated garage, then got out, motioning me to put my car next to hers. We went in through the laundry room.

"Did Richard follow you? Could you tell?"

It hadn't occurred to me, so I hadn't been looking. She unlocked the door and, once we were inside, chained it and set the burglar alarm. The apartment was a duplex, dirty shag carpet, peeling purple wallpaper—the furniture, she was quick to tell me, wasn't hers, and included an upright piano. She lifted the piano lid and took out a pill vial. Inside were a half dozen joints—she lit one.

"You sure?" I said. She seemed fairly paranoid

already. I watched her peer through the drapes.

"Oh shit," she said.

"Come on, he's not out there."

But he was. The gold Lexus was at the curb, and Richard was sitting behind the wheel. He was lighting a cigarette.

"I gotta calm down," she said. She took some brandy out of a cabinet and poured herself a glass. "You?"

"No, thank you." I was feeling light-headed enough.

She nodded. "Does he strike you as a guy who owns a gun?"

"Richard?" I said. She was at the window again. "I'd be surprised if Richard owned a flyswatter."

"Well, he belongs to a gun club. He owns a bunch of guns."

I shrugged. "I don't know why that doesn't scare me."

She was somewhat relieved to hear that. "He took me to the shooting range once. The whole corny routine, putting his arm around me, showing me how to hold the gun, the pistol, whatever you call it, pressing up against me. Creeped me out. You like my hair this way?"

"Yeah, I think it's great." She was starting to get a new buzz.

"Because I was thinking of cutting it even shorter and going all blonde."

"Personally?" I said. "I don't think you can ever go wrong."

"You are the sweetest."

She kissed me. The Lexus was still out there—she peered out at it again, chewing her lip, smiling. I came over and pulled her away. She kissed me harder. "You're my knight in shining armor," she said.

"Mm-hmm," I said—though actually I felt funny being there in the living room, just one door between us and the gold Lexus. But we were already on the couch.

"What else would you do for me?"

"I'm doing it," I said, helping her off with her top.

"If I didn't let you in, would you break down my door?"

I didn't get the reference—or maybe she didn't mean anything by it.

"What's the matter? I bet you would."

I was looking at her body. There was something meaty about her after all—big thighs, pudgy belly, though her arms were fairly skinny. "Yeah," I said. "Whatever."

"I bet you could get any girl you wanted."

She liked to talk during sex—so be it. "Yeah, but I want you."

"You like these? You like little breasts?"

"I like yours," I said. Her nipples were large and brown—she ran her thumbs over them.

"Girls with little tits," she said, "like boys with big dicks."

The walls fell away as I kissed her—I felt myself spin out into the darkness, as if to check on Richard in the gold Lexus, and then I heard it, saw it, pulling away from the curb. We were on the couch now, and Richard's car was gone—I was picturing him returning to his house, barging past the party guests up to his room, rummaging through his gun collection. Whoa, I told myself, you didn't see that, you're spooking yourself, and I banished Richard Nesbit from my mind, focusing instead on Gwen, the smell

rising from her body. We made love for an hour, first
on the couch, then upstairs in a fourposter bed that
almost filled her bedroom, and a mirror on the wall
or on the closet doors—I could see myself pumping
away, for what felt like longer than an hour, but
that's what the clock said when I looked at it again.
She never came, not that I noticed, but that didn't
seem to bother her. She kept searching my face with
her eyes, head going back and forth on the pillow.
"You're my hero," she said, more than once. I fell
asleep inside her and woke up in the middle of the
night. She was still asleep. I padded downstairs naked
and peered out the front window. The Lexus was
gone. When I got back upstairs, she was staring at
the canopy ceiling.

"I *am* going to lose the store," she said.

"Shh," I said, getting back into bed.

"I can't make my insurance payments. I can't pay
the rent-a-cops. My head hurts," she said.

She was crashing. I stroked her hair. "What about
Richard?"

"Yes, he'll help me. If I marry him."

"You could always hock the ring," I said lightly.

She shook her head. "He'd kill me. And I can't
get enough for my car."

I closed my eyes. Her voice droned on, chipper
and frightened, like a flight recording.

"—and I need to broaden my inventory."

I got up again, this time to piss, thinking about her
frustration, wishing I could help somehow. My head
was starting to ache, too, as though her pain was
contagious. Through the bathroom door I looked
back at her lying naked under the canopy. For an
instant I thought I saw a tattoo on her thigh, like on
Sandra Loyacano's—right away a spear went through

my heart. A lizard tattoo? Your eyes are playing tricks on you, I thought—I looked closer and of course, that's all it was.

"—Shit!" I gasped.

"What is it? Denny?"

I was back in bed.

"What happened?" she said.

I opened my eyes. "Did I just get up to pee?"

"No," she said.

The bathroom door was closed. I reached and kicked it open with my foot. Her bag was sitting there on the counter, her wallet was poking out the top and a pale blue diaphragm case was lying on the counter.

"Denny?" she said.

I lay back on the pillow, turned my head to the mirror on the closet doors, where I'd watched us making love. But of course there was no mirror— there or anywhere in the room.

"Are you okay with everything?" she said. "You're not gonna get cold feet?"

Cold feet? "I'm fine," I said.

"I knew it," she said. "I knew it the minute I laid eyes on you."

Knew what? I sniffed the air, as though smelling would help me remember. "What about Richard?"

"What about him?"

"Is he here?"

"Is he back?" she said. She laughed. "What do you mean?"

"His car." My mind was a blank.

"I don't know, you want to look out the window?"

She started to nibble at my chest. I rolled on top of her, and she tightened. "Denny," she warned me, and reached over and opened her night table drawer.

I tore a condom off a roll, put it on, then walked to
the window for a real look. No gold Lexus, no Richard Nesbit with a gun. I climbed back into bed. When
I entered her again, she gave a little squeak of gratitude.

The minute I laid eyes on you?

"Are you always this dependable?" she said
sweetly.

"So they tell me," I said. We started moving.

"—It's like you're not really here?"

"What?" I said suddenly.

"Oh, that's so nice," she said. "Don't stop. That's
great. You *promise*?"

Promise what?

"I promise," I heard myself say. She thanked me
with a kiss. I watched our mouths grind together,
trying to make sense of it, while our bodies sank
below me, vanishing slowly into the darkness.

7

Something serious had happened, something not covered by Randy Nelson's test.

I tried not to think about it, but that was like not thinking of an elephant. Watching basketball on Sunday with Elliot, I replayed the entire night in my head, Gwen's tongue in my mouth, slamming Richard's head against the pool-shed wall, Richard screaming threats at Gwen, the talk about his gun club, everything I could remember and all the things I couldn't.

Elliot wanted to know about the party. "What happened? Who was there?"

"It was okay," was all I said. "Bunch of snobs." What else was I leaving out? Thinking for a second Gwen was Sandra Loyacano, the promise I didn't want to know about, when had I made that, when I was chasing Richard Nesbit in my head? To save my life I couldn't fill in the gaps. When I made a food run for Mimi, and a cop car passed me going the other way, I half expected it to make a U-turn and pull me over. For what? I didn't have a clue.

All I knew was, I was scared to go to work on Monday. I tried to call Gwen but her number was unlisted, and I'd forgotten to write down the address—it was so dark that night I didn't remember a house number. As it happened, Simon Lefcourt didn't come by the job site till Tuesday. I thought of asking him for Gwen's phone number, but I didn't follow through on that. I was trying to avoid him and I didn't know why.

Then, as I was counting my poker winnings after work, Simon Lefcourt ambled up behind me and asked me into his office. He shooed Boris out and we were sitting there alone, across a beat-up metal desk piled with plans.

"Boris says you're doing good work," he said.

"Thank you, sir." I should have been relieved, but I wasn't. He was still measuring me.

"How much college have you had, Denton?"

"Just one year," I said.

"How come?" he asked. "You're obviously a very bright guy."

I nodded. "I don't know," I said. "I guess I wanted to be the first in my family not to graduate."

He didn't find that amusing. "There's got to be more to it than that," he said.

What did he care? First Randy, I thought, now Simon. "There wasn't enough money," I said, "after a certain point."

"Well listen," he said. "In my opinion, a garage mechanic is a physicist who never got his degree."

For some reason he was determined to think well of me. Did he know I'd been with his daughter Friday night?

"This is going to sound a little weird, Denton."

Here it comes, I thought.

"I'm about to bid on a job," he said. "And I wanted to get your input."

Input? "Sure," I said.

"It's a contract," he said, "to build a prison."

I nodded. I was thinking about Gwen—I saw her breezing into her store, big smile on her face.

"Prison design hasn't changed in two hundred years."

"Really," I said. "I didn't know." I was trying to look interested, but my mind was definitely on Gwen.

"Did you know America invented the penitentiary?"

"No, I didn't," I said.

"The atom bomb and the prison, two of our major cultural exports. You know who built the first one?"

"The first atomic bomb?"

"The first prison."

"No, sir," I said.

"The Quakers. Benjamin Franklin."

"Well," I said, "it stands to reason."

That seemed to tickle him. "Yes it does, doesn't it. The Quakers only *thought* they were liberals. Really, they wanted the bad guys cooped up and tortured, instead of wandering the countryside. They just pretended they were building monasteries."

"Yeah," I said, "that's right." I was getting a little lost.

"So when are you seeing Gwen again?" he said.

At this I snapped to attention, thinking he was referring to the party—then I recalled he had seen me leave with her the day we went to lunch. "I don't know," I said. "I haven't spoken to Gwen in a while."

He nodded again, like I'd just told him something he needed to know.

"So can I buy you a cup of coffee sometime? And we'll talk about prison design."

"I'll look forward to that," I said.

My head was still buzzing as I walked to my car—the smile on Gwen's face, her voice in my ear asking me to help her out, but how or why I couldn't remember, the handle was just out of reach, like I was trying to recall a word but didn't know what letter it began with, and now here was Simon sucking up to me for no good reason.

I drove home, showered, changed, and reported to the main house. Elliot was late for dinner. I made myself a drink—there were some books on adoption in the living room, brand-new. I drank my drink and pictured Gwen locking up her store. Another half hour passed and still Elliot wasn't here, and by the time he did arrive, dinner, according to Mimi, was spoiled.

We ate mostly in silence, me waiting for some random clue that would help things fall into place.

"I checked out Simon Lefcourt," Elliot said as Mimi was getting the coffee. "I went down to Groman Lumber, and I asked if he paid his bills by the tenth. And guess what they told me."

"What?"

"He doesn't. He drives a Caddy, but he's broke. His ex-wife took him to the cleaners."

"Who told you that? I don't believe it," I said, as Mimi came back into the dining room.

"His daughter owns a store in Renton," said Elliot.

"Yes, I've been there," I said.

"You have."

"On a job," I said.

My voice must have sounded funny, because he gave me a fishy look. "Well, she's behind in her insurance payments."

My radar went on alert. "How do you know that?"

Elliot looked at me over his coffee. "I know the people who insure her."

"I see," I said. "Small world."

"Guess what I found in the mailbox today," Mimi piped up.

"What," said Elliot.

"A dog turd," said Mimi. And she smiled a fake smile.

"Fuck," said Elliot under his breath. "Who put it there?"

"I don't know," said Mimi dryly. "The turd didn't have a note wrapped around it."

They were itching for a fight, not with me, with each other. "Look," I said quickly, "I told you I'd be out of your hair, and I will be."

"Be quiet," Elliot said. "Both of you. We don't know it has anything to do with Denton living here."

"Oh, what else would it mean," said Mimi.

"The dog-walker," said Elliot. "I wouldn't put it past her, what's her IQ, about fifty?"

"It wasn't April," said Mimi.

"Oh, how do you know," said Elliot, and they started bickering in earnest. Suddenly I felt sleepy, thinking, if somebody was looking in the window now, would they still think we were a solid family? No, because I could see Mimi and Elliot barking at each other. Then a shadow seemed to fall across my eyes, like somebody was blocking my view of the dining room, April Hartigan or some other nosy neighbor, and when my vision cleared I was no longer at the table, just Elliot and Mimi, arguing so heatedly they hadn't seen me leave the room. All at once I felt grass and gravel under my feet—as I started across the driveway, I heard the back door to the main house bang open and there was Elliot running after me.

"Denton, come back. I'm sorry."

I kept right on going. "Give me two weeks, I'll be out of here."

"Mimi doesn't mean it. She doesn't mean what she's saying."

"For your information," I said, "I had a talk with Simon Lefcourt today. He's bidding on a prison contract and he wants my advice. I don't give a shit what Groman Lumber says, the guy's a good guy, he knows I'm dating his daughter—"

"So you *are* dating Gwen Lefcourt. I thought so. Do you want to hear what I heard about *her*?"

"No," I said. I burst into the garage and up the stairs.

"You know how many schools she went to? Five. Three different rehabs. Every ex-con who comes through her father's door, she ends up screwing them, okay?"

"Boy, you really have done your homework, haven't you? I guess I shouldn't ask her to dinner, huh?"

"You asked her to dinner? Without consulting us?"

"Elliot, I'm joking, take it easy—"

"I don't want her in my house. And I don't want her messing with your head."

"Fine, you've made your point. Listen, if you and Mimi are having problems, why don't you deal with it, stop blaming me, stop blaming Gwen Lefcourt. She's no Mother Teresa, but she's got a good heart, so lay off."

I slammed the door on him and fell into a chair.

All of a sudden I felt foolish. Dating her? I didn't even have her phone number. Where was she? Had we made arrangements to meet? Where was Richard Nesbit, was he making trouble? I could picture him pacing through his parents' house, and I started to be afraid for Gwen—I ought to try and find his house again, confront him. Gwen was there right now, I was sure of it, making excuses for Friday night—I could see him moving behind his blinds, following her from room to room, getting uglier by the second. She was trying to make it to the front door and I was trying to get between them, grab him by the throat and put my fist through his teeth. He picked up a lamp, taunting her with it, then slammed it back down and seized her by the hair. I reared back and swung at him with all my might.

I rolled over in bed.

I was dead awake. Daylight was streaming into my room, the pigeons were cooing, Ozzie was barking.

I went in to brush my teeth.

That's when I became aware of the blood—there was a tiny smear of it across my forehead. On each of the knuckles of my right hand was a scab—they must have opened up just now, when I was lying in bed, running my fist across my face.

I went back into the bedroom. Sure enough, there was blood on my pillow, and a tiny spot on the sheet. I started to panic, sat down again, got a grip. From my window I could see Elliot in the kitchen—he was looking out the window toward the garage. I saw him get up and go to the back door—I hurried downstairs and across the lawn.

"Morning," he said.

He was making coffee. For a minute he didn't say anything, and then came the question I was dreading.

"Where'd you go last night?"

I poured myself some orange juice, keeping my scabby hand out of sight, trying not to panic. "Out," I said.

"Your therapist called," he said.

My heart jumped. "When?"

"After you left. Apparently you missed a session."

I downed the orange juice. "Jesus," I said.

"Tuesdays and Fridays. Do you need me to remind you every time? Where are you going?"

"To call her," I said. I went back to the garage and dialed Randy's number.

"She's in session," the receptionist told me.

The line went dead a moment. Then Randy came on.

"Dr. Nelson, I'm sorry, I forgot."

"Mr. Hake, if you can't keep our appointments—"

"No, please don't tell Ortega. I'll make up the time," I said. "Please."

"I have a twelve and I have a one, which would you prefer?"

I was trapped. "One," I said, and hung up. I stripped the bed, knotting the blood-stained sheet and the pillowcase into the smallest bundle I could. I waited until I heard Elliot's car pull out, then headed to my car with my dirty laundry. I tossed the bundle in the back, started to get behind the wheel. April Hartigan was coming down the sidewalk in her Loden coat, trailing her empty dog leash behind her. I started up the car but it was too late, she'd seen me.

"Blessings," she said, staring at me with her monkey eyes.

"Have a nice day," I said, thinking why does she rub me the wrong way? Because, I decided, at least she knows where she is all the time, no matter how much her life sucks she has the courage to be around while it's going on. Me, I was zoning out so completely I missed my exit—that, plus having to stop by the linen store for new sheets and pillowcases, same brand, same shade of yellow, made me an hour late for work. Boris swooped down on my car as I pulled in.

"Yeah, I know," I said. My hand was still throbbing. "I'm sorry."

"Listen," he said, "I don't care whose ass you're kissing, you get here on time—"

I was putting on my work gloves, glad to hide the scabs. "Lighten up, okay?"

"Lend me fifty bucks, I'll forget it."

"I don't have it," I said. My heart was going a mile a minute.

"Come on, you know you're just gonna win it back."

I took out my wallet, dread rising in my throat, the way it does when you know you've left your wallet someplace, only I was expecting to find more than I wanted to. I was expecting to find my wallet bulging with bills. It wasn't—just a few twenties, the extra cash I'd gotten at the grocery store, minus ten dollars or so. Relieved, I handed Boris two twenties and a ten, shoved the wallet back in my pocket. Simon Lefcourt's Caddy was pulling into the lot. I picked up a cement-spreader and started to work, and then I saw Simon heading my way.

"I need to talk to you," he said.

"Sure. Okay," I said. He was pacing back and forth, very agitated—Gwen's Cherokee was pulling up outside the construction gate. I watched her get out and walk with her dad toward the shed. She was practically in tears. I saw him reach for the phone and give her a card from his wallet, then look through his Rolodex and come up with a number. It had nothing to do with me, I was praying to God it didn't.

A minute later she came out of the shed. She saw me looking and started to hurry up toward her Cherokee—she didn't want to talk, or rather she didn't want to be seen talking to me, that's what I gathered from the warning glance she gave me. Simon wasn't watching, so I sidled up beside her.

"You okay?" I said. "What's the matter?"

She shot another glance toward the shed. "I can't talk now." She started to get into her vehicle—I put a hand on her arm.

"You were with Richard last night."

Her eyes widened. "Yes. Yes, that's right."

I winced. "Why did you go there?"

Her voice dropped to a whisper. "How did you know I went to his house?"

I was searching her face for bruises. "At least he didn't draw blood."

"What do you mean, draw blood?"

I shoved my fist deeper in my pocket. She got into the Cherokee.

"Goodbye," she said, and then: "I'll call you." She started to put the Cherokee in gear and then she stopped.

"When did you talk to Richard? I have to know."

"I didn't—"

"Then how did you know he hit me?"

I felt my skin go cold. "I was watching through the window."

"When? You couldn't have."

"I saw him pick up a lamp. I saw him grab you by the hair."

"No way," she said. She closed her eyes and opened them.

"I wanted to kill him."

"But there's a gate around the house—it has motion detectors—"

She broke off—her dad was calling to me from the shed. Without another word Gwen backed the Cherokee out of the lot. I watched her go, then trotted toward the shed. Simon was behind his desk, eyes closed, kneading his forehead. When he saw me come in, he sat up quickly in his chair. I braced myself.

"Denton," he said, "do you know how to read blueprints?"

"Blueprints? Yes, sir." My head was reeling.

"Take a look at these." He twisted one of the sets of plans so they were facing me, started pointing with his pencil. "These are the cellblocks. These are the towers. You see these two-room cells, you see how they're laid out, you think that could fly?"

"I'm sorry, two-room cells?" There were initials in the corner of the plans, RN, Richard Nesbit—I was trying desperately to focus.

"Did Gwen speak to you just now?"

I tightened. "Yes, sir. We said hello."

He eyed me. "She didn't tell you?"

"No. Tell me what?"

"Her store was broken into last night."

The floor tilted under my feet. "Whoa," I said softly.

"That's right."

"That's horrible." My head was buzzing like a chain saw. "What did they get?"

"You've been over to her store, right?"

"Yes, sir. I put up that wall for you, remember?"

He frowned, as though this was something he'd successfully forgotten. "Yes, of course," he said.

"How did they get in?" I asked.

For a second he didn't answer—just looked at my face. "Punched in the back window."

My scabs throbbed inside my gloves. "Uh-huh," I said. "What about the alarm?"

"What alarm," he said.

"I thought I saw a system," I said. "Yes, in fact, I know I did." Shut up, I thought.

"She forgot to pay her security bill," he said.

"Jesus," I said.

"Jewelry," he said. "She had way too much on display."

"Did she. I didn't notice." You're not that stupid, I was thinking. You would've wrapped my hand in a towel before busting that window.

"All right, so let me ask you something."

But your head was miles away, I thought. "Yes, sir," I said. You were in Oaktree Estates, spying on Richard Nesbit.

"If you could make one change in prison design, what would it be?"

"In prison design?" I said. I was lost.

"From the standpoint of discipline. Motivating people to change their lives, like the Founding Fathers intended."

So we were back to the blueprints. "I don't know," I said, flustered. "I could try and think about it."

He scowled suddenly. "You must think I'm a fool, don't you."

"No, sir."

"My daughter's store gets broken into, and here I'm talking about trying to rehabilitate criminals."

"No, not at all." He was staring at me oddly, like he saw right through me and was afraid to say so.

"Total surveillance," I said suddenly.

"In what sense."

"Cameras in every cell. Make the prisoners earn their privacy."

"All right, exactly. That's exactly the concept here," he said, tapping the plans with his knuckle. "Good time for good behavior. You ever been to an Italian monastery?"

"No, sir, just Canada." I hardly knew what I was saying.

"You'd be amazed how some of those monks lived. Three-room suites, bigger than any room my daughter had at college." He refolded the plans, nodding to himself—then, so low I almost didn't hear him, he said, "The thing is, a convicted felon, the police may want to talk to you about the break-in."

"I understand," I said. I was picturing Felix Ortega in his office, reading a fax of the arrest log, and I knew I had to see Randy. I couldn't wait for one o'clock. "I wouldn't do anything to hurt your daughter," I said.

"Of course you didn't. I wasn't suggesting that."

"Is it okay if I go to lunch a little early?"

"Sure. I understand. Your parole officer will probably want reassurances. To be continued," he said, and waved me toward the door. In a daze I went down the steps, past Boris and the other guys pouring cement. My scabs burned. I tossed off my work gloves, got into my car.

I drove the thirty miles to Randy Nelson's office in a cold sweat. It was a little before eleven when I got there—I sat in the parking lot for a while, trying to compose myself, then went inside the building and up to the desk.

"I have a one o'clock with Dr. Nelson. But if she's here, I'd like to see her."

I sat back down. The receptionist got on the phone, and a minute later Randy appeared at the head of the stairway.

"We don't have a lot of time," she said. "My next client's due any minute."

"I appreciate this," I said. I went into her office, sat in the chair, hands in my lap. She took a sheet of paper off her desk.

"Your test results," she said. "Would you like to hear?"

"I don't know, would I?"

"You tested high," she said.

"For what?"

"Dissociative experiences."

I played dumb—Dull Normal. "That doesn't mean antisocial."

"No. We're talking about fugue states. Amnesias."

I looked at my hand, the scabs. "That's hardly news."

"Denton, it's nothing to be ashamed of. Everybody spaces out to some degree."

"To some degree," I said.

"Actors. Artists. Therapists. It's called having an imagination."

"Thieves?" I said, looking at her carefully.

I saw her breathe in sharply. "What's the emergency?" she said.

I couldn't make my mouth work. I was going to make her pry it out of me.

"Why did you miss the last session?"

I was staring out the window, watching the breeze stir the trees.

"I've been thinking a lot about my dad's death." As soon as I said it, I wondered why—it didn't seem to be true, just something she would want to hear, something to keep me from talking about Gwen and the burglary.

"What about it?"

"See, what nobody understands, what my brother Elliot doesn't understand, they loved each other. He could be miserable to her but she loved him and he loved her. They used to talk in their sleep, she told me that, my mom. One would speak and the other would answer."

"In what way was he miserable to her?"

"He cheated on her," I said. I realized I was picking at my scabs, and I stopped. "That's what Elliot says, anyhow. I was too young to see the signs. The day he shot himself his nurse, Dot, kept calling him up on the phone. And he and Mom were fighting. I think I remember she was packing, threatening to leave. And then he went down to the cellar."

Why did I rush over here, I thought.

"I don't really know why he killed himself," I said. "It never made any sense to me."

She nodded toward my lap. "What happened to your hand?" she said. Who was I kidding, I thought, she saw the scabs right away. "Did you get into a fight?"

I was trying to stay calm. "No. I don't know. I told you, my body's one place and my mind's another. Fugue states, okay, that sounds right. A big jumble where you can't hear the melody. Like trying to grab smoke out of the air." Randy was nodding—

she liked the sound of that. "I don't know what brings it on. When I'm tense."

"Conflicted."

"The way my mind works. Conflicted, yes, okay."

"And then you start to act out."

"You mean I lose control. Of my impulses. Sure, I guess that's what it looks like to you."

"You realize how fast you've been talking?"

"Am I? No." The tree branches waved beyond the window. "It's sort of happening now. I'm here but I'm out there," I said.

"You're in two places at once."

"More or less. Yeah. Like if you were listening to me and thinking what to cook for dinner. In that sense, only more. More serious."

"Did this happen last night?"

"I don't know. Yes. I was asleep. I knew Gwen was at Richard Nesbit's house."

"Gwen is the girl you met."

"Yes. Richard Nesbit is her boyfriend. Ex-boyfriend. He's dangerous, he's a gun freak. He was beating up on her," I said, unable to stop myself—between her poker face and the pressure I was feeling, it was like we were both someplace else. "Gwen's store was broken into last night," I heard myself say, and then: "I think maybe it was done for the insurance."

"What makes you say that?"

"She needed cash. Her insurance was about to run out."

Randy nodded slowly. "Did she ask you to rob her store?"

"I think so. Yes. But that doesn't mean I did it," I said. I could hear the resentment in my voice, I could feel my mind slipping away—flashing, now, on Sandra Loyacano. She was getting out of her mom's car, the two-seater Mercedes, license plate 4SADIE, carrying a Benneton bag.

"If I put you under hypnosis, do you think last night might come back to you?"

"Yeah, it might," I said.

"Do you want to try it?"

"No," I said. "No, I don't."

"Why not?"

I tried to focus, but all I could see was Sandra Loyacano. I was inside her house, she was giving me a tour—she picked up a vase and tossed it at me.

"Denton?" I heard Randy say, "why don't you want to be hypnotized?"

Good thing you caught it, she was saying. You'd owe my mom ten thousand dollars. I sat up in the chair.

"Because," I said, "I could say anything, and I wouldn't know it, and if the cops came to you, you'd have to tell them."

"No, I wouldn't."

"Bullshit. None of this is confidential. All this can be subpoenaed—"

"Denton, that's just not true—"

"Okay, you know what else I hate? When people try to one-up you by using your name, like when they pat you on the back. In the joint, the guards could touch you but you couldn't touch the guards? That says it all, as far as I'm concerned. I'm sorry I said anything, okay? I'll check out if your client is here and I'll send them up, okay? I've gotta get back to my job."

"Mr. Hake, sit down—"

"Now it's Mr. Hake. You have *no* idea what's

going on,'' I said, halfway out the door. ''I'm not saying *I* do, but you don't. This is nothing you've ever seen before. I'm not evil. I don't mean to hurt people, I'm not violent by nature. I'm a good person, I'm not a thief.''

''Then why are you running?'' I heard her say, but I was already out in the hall, hurrying down the stairs and through the lobby and into my car. I pictured Randy getting on the phone and calling Ortega and the next thing I knew I thought the car behind me was Ortega's, and it wasn't even close to looking like Ortega's car. All afternoon I kept my eyes peeled for his gray Dodge, but he didn't show up, and Gwen didn't return, and Simon didn't call me back into his office—he was off at another site. My mind kept wandering, from Gwen to Richard to Randy and then to Sandra Loyacano again—I put up three rows of metal shelving without giving it a thought, working faster and better than I'd worked since Simon hired me. Boris even asked me to slow down—I was making everybody nervous. I asked to go home early, and he let me punch out. I walked to my car, got inside, and sat there.

That lying little bitch, I was thinking. You didn't break into her house. You were there by invitation.

I put the car in gear, driving all the way home before I remembered to get rid of the blood-stained pillowcase and sheets—then I thought, stupid, just put the bundle in the trash. Mimi wasn't home yet—I did a wash, put the new yellow sheets and pillowcases in the machine so they wouldn't look stiff on the bed, in case Mimi came snooping around.

The phone rang. I picked it up—there was nothing but a dial tone. Faintly, I heard a second ring, coming from the garage. It rang five times and kept on ringing. I went out the back door and up the stairs to my room. The phone rang a seventh time, and an eighth. I locked the door and picked it up.

"Hello?" I said.

"Hake, it's Ortega."

I took a deep breath. "Everything's okay," I said. "I saw my shrink today, we're up to date."

"That's not what I'm calling about."

I steeled myself.

"Your case is up for review," he said.

"Already?" I said. My voice sounded cold and faraway. "That's great," I said.

"I have to ask you something," he said.

My throat tightened up. "What?"

"That guy you work for. Simon Lefcourt. There was a robbery at his daughter's store."

"Yes, I know," I said.

"Would you know anything about that?"

In my mind's eye I was seeing Sandra Loyacano, the two of us splashing naked in her parents' pool. "Only what I heard from Simon."

"I had to ask you that," he said. "You understand why."

"I understand completely," I said.

"You know," he said, "you could've waited till your parole was up. Instead of making me look bad like this."

I heard a smile in his voice. "Sir, I'm going to assume you're kidding."

"And I'm going to assume you're telling me the truth," he said, "until the police tell me different."

"I appreciate that," I said. "Thank you." The phone clicked off and I hung up the receiver, still picturing Sandra Loyacano. We were in a bedroom now, green shag rug and satin pillows. You're not making this up, I thought, you had sex in the pool, then in her parents' mirrored bedroom—you left a wet spot on the carpet and your hair in the sheets.

And then you robbed her.

So how do you know you didn't rob Gwen?

If you didn't punch in Gwen's window, how did your knuckles get bloody?

A door opened and banged shut. I looked out the window and saw Elliot coming across the lawn.

"Dinner's ready," he called up through the window. Then I heard him coming up the stairs. I undid the latch, stuck my hands in my pockets. He was smiling for some reason. "Good news?" I said.

"I had a good day," he said. "I wrote three hundred K."

"That's good, Elliot."

"You know what the monthly average is? I made that in four hours."

"You must be feeling better," I said. My scabby hand was still hidden.

"I am. I just wanted you to know. Mimi and I decided to go for counseling. We're fighting in front of you and that's not right."

"Elliot, it's okay. You're trying to deal with it, I understand."

"I meant what I said about Gwen Lefcourt. She's not for you." He turned toward the house—Mimi was calling him. "*What*?" he shouted back, throwing open the shutters. I couldn't hear what she was saying—Elliot closed the shutters again.

"Somebody at the door," he said. "If you want a drink before dinner, you'd better come up to the house now."

"Okay," I said, edging toward the window. I

could make out two figures coming up the walk, and a vehicle beyond.

It was a cop car, city of Auburn.

I felt my mind go up the flue. I went totally cold.

I looked again and saw Elliot in the living room, bullshitting with two cops and Mimi coming out the back door toward the garage.

I was downstairs in a flash. Mimi met me in the driveway.

"They want to talk to you. Elliot said you weren't here."

"Jesus, why. I'll talk to them. What do they want?"

"I don't know, Denton. I thought maybe *you* knew. Where are you going?"

"If he said I'm not here, I'd better not be here. Get a number, I'll call them as soon as I get in."

"Where are you going?"

"For a ride, okay?" I must have snapped at her without meaning to, because she reared back suddenly and trotted toward the house, whether to fetch Elliot or not I wasn't sticking around to find out. I vaulted the fence and ran to my car, jumped in, did a 180 and headed up the street, pedal to the floor. The next thing I knew I was on the Interstate and then five miles were gone like that and then another five miles, whoosh, like an invisible hand had picked up the car and dropped it ten miles away. My heart was racing and my mind was everywhere, but I knew where I was now, I was in Renton—I looked out the window and there it was, the mini-mall, Gwen's store, a square of plywood masking the back window and the lights on and the sign in the front window, CLOSED FOR INVENTORY. Gwen was inside, the jewelry cases were empty and a bunch of people drifting back and forth, fat ladies, customers, insurance people, I hadn't the faintest idea. Gwen was gazing out toward the alley and she must have seen my car, because a moment later there she was coming out the back door. I thought I saw her wave my car away, but I couldn't be sure. I was out of there.

You didn't do it, I told myself. Then I thought: they fucked you back then, they'll fuck you now.

I floored it.

I was thinking all the places they couldn't follow me—Randy's office, Canada. The light ahead of me turned yellow.

I leaned on the horn. A shape hurtled toward me, smacked the side of the car. I saw my Nova spin and continue to spin, three times around, saw it from a great height. A third car plowed into my fender. Now my Nova was still, my head was on the wheel and the horn was sounding. I heard sirens. I heard myself breathing. I heard a moan come out of my mouth. Then I heard nothing at all.

PART TWO

8

I couldn't move my fingers, I couldn't turn my head. People were bending over me. I could hear them clanking around like boulders bumping underwater, and I wanted to tell them to stop, stop moving, stop poking me, but my mouth wouldn't work, even when I could see them.

Then everything went dim again. Shadows came and went, without bothering me one way or the other. There was a tube down my throat, wires sprouting from my chest and head, computer screens everywhere. The room smelled of flowers, so many different kinds I couldn't pick out a scent. From where I was watching I could hear music trickling out of a tape recorder by my bed, bands Elliot and I used to listen to, Van Morrison, Treat Her Right, plus some singer I didn't recognize, a woman. I could see the room, I *was* the room—the room had eyes and ears and they were plugged into my brain, my brain and the room were painted on the outside of a bubble and I was inside looking out, watching the green spikes of the heart monitor drift across a black screen.

Then suddenly I was noplace again, sucked back into the blackness of myself, with just the faintest light seeping through my skin and skull, a warmth, a pressure, a sign of something out there trying to get in.

Me, I thought.

A doctor was shining a light in my eye. I felt it in the back of my head, a pinprick of pain that flared out across the inside of my skull. And then I was gone again. Some clock was pulsing deep inside my head, I knew time was passing, but everything was black light, somebody pleading with me, myself or my mom. She was sitting there below me in the chair, squeezing my hand with both hands, Elliot across the bed from her, watching, while a doctor circled the bed.

"He's got all his reflexes."

It was true, I could see my pupil shrinking—my eyes were open and I was looking into them. Mom was in the room, and Gwen, and Mimi, there was Simon Lefcourt in the corridor, waiting, and the nurse shooing everybody out. Then waves of silence washed over me. I was on my back again looking out, trying to figure out what time of day it was, black space rolling under me, no vertical, no horizontal, just floating. Elliot was coming in with sandwiches. I sat up to eat, but no, there I was below me, still lying there. The music was still playing. The room was full of nurses and students.

"—No skull fracture, no hemorrhage, and how do we know that?"

"No blood in the cerebrospinal fluid."

"Intracranial pressure?"

"Not elevated. Heart rate under sixty, respiration slow, blood pressure low."

"So what are we seeing here?"

"One thing, his body temperature fluctuates between ninety-six and ninety-nine."

"Can anyone account for this?"

Did anybody call Ortega?

I watched the students file out below me. Then Elliot and Mom were sitting beside me again.

"Come on, pal, we know you're in there."

Elliot, I'm over here.

"Denton?"

I was gliding along the ceiling, I was curling around their ankles like a cat. Sometimes the voices were like the wind, sometimes clear as a bell.

"Here's one you like."

I watched from above as he turned the music up.

"Elliot, he moved."

"He's fine. They say he's gonna be fine."

"Why does he do these things?"

"Please, the guy rammed him broadside. Denton?"

Elliot crept close. I saw him take the flesh of my forearm between his fingers and give it a twist.

"Come on. I know you feel that. Stop playing possum, you crazy bastard."

I slid along the walls, across the ceiling and down again, until I found a windowpane. Rain was pouring down. I floated back past Elliot, trying to get in his ear, but as soon as I got close, everything swam away, like furniture bobbing on a flood.

I'm here, God damn it.

Somebody pressed my arm. I looked down and saw Gwen Lefcourt sitting by my bed. Her hair was lemon-yellow.

"I hate the red-eye. I'd rather fly halfway round the world than take the red-eye."

And she sobbed. She put her hand to her face, then took it away, shook her head violently, stood up from the bed beside her father.

"Gwen honey. Why don't we go."

"He's not even sick, there's nothing broken."

"His brother's back, I think he'd just as soon he didn't see us." Simon Lefcourt had his hand under her elbow and they were moving toward the corridor. By and by Elliot came in again.

"Denny, you missed a major rainstorm."

Elliot, I heard it.

"I called Ortega, everything's fine with that, don't worry. Hey, you want to get mad? I found more dog-shit in the mailbox."

My head lolled. I heard the chair scrape back as Elliot fell into it, cursing—the ICU nurse tapped him on the shoulder. Shapes were moving beyond the glass, Elliot and two other guys, one with a big head like a beet, the other with a small head like a potato. I tried to focus but the light was too bright and then I realized it was leaking through the window, etching it like acid until there was nothing but a sheet of light across my brain.

"I went through all this with the other officers."

Through all what? Elliot and the two men were moving away down the hall.

"I don't know Carl Williams, I never met the man, I never took a call from Carl Williams. To the best of my knowledge, Carl Williams has never tried to contact my brother."

Carl Williams?

"—My brother has his own phone line, it's none of my business."

"Was he aware that Carl Williams escaped? Did he ever mention it?"

"Never."

"Would you mind if we played back your brother's answering machine?"

Is that who they were looking for, Carl? Then what was I doing on my back?

"Don't you guys talk to each other? I gave his answering machine tape to the Auburn police. Listen, my brother did his time, he earned his parole, he's been a model parolee and was about to be discharged, he has everything to live for—"

"We're not accusing him of any crime."

They're not accusing you, I thought. They didn't find your blood at the store, you were never *at* the store that night.

"Then what else do you want me to do?"

Through the glass I saw the monitors spiking. I saw my mouth open. Elliot!

"—Excuse me, fellas, I need to get back to my brother."

They were moving below me, two nurses and an orderly, Elliot behind them, and a doctor, all hurrying into my room. The light behind my eyes drained away. My eyes ached from dryness. My joints swelled with pain. I could see them all around my bed.

"Blood pressure one thirty over seventy."

"We're getting fast delta here—"

"His heart rate's up, he's breathing fast."

"Guys, feel his skin. It's warm again."

The room went dark, then light. My brother's face rose above me.

"Denton?"

I blinked my eyes.

"You're back, pal."

My jaw was stiff, every muscle in my body was sore, my lips felt like cracked rubber.

"What did he just say?" asked Elliot. The doctor took the light out of my eye. I felt massively weak, like a newborn baby worn out from crying.

"Do you know where you are?"

"Carn. Carnon. Carlton Municipal."

"That's right." The doctor—he had a goatee—shot a look at Elliot. "Do you know how long you've been here?"

I could only guess. "Couple few days."

"You remember why?"

"I tried to run a light," I said. "Who else was hurt?"

"Nobody," said Elliot, and I blacked out. When I opened my eyes again I was in a semi-private room. The monitors were gone, and there was a screen between me and a woman in the next bed. They wheeled me down the hall and into the elevator and shoved me lengthwise into a long tube that echoed like a garbage can when they zapped my head. When I got back to my room, there was Elliot and Mom.

Mom hugged me. "Don't feel bad. I didn't feel bad."

"God told you not to worry," I said.

"That's right," she said. "And don't mock it."

"I'm not mocking. I'm grateful." They gave me a walker and we went up and down the corridor, Elliot behind us. I was remembering Gwen in the ICU, her hand on my arm. "So you met my girlfriend," I said.

Elliot frowned. "When did she call you?"

"She didn't," I said. I was waiting for him to ask how I knew Gwen had been here, but he didn't.

"Well, *I* thought she was adorable," said Mom. "And her father has been *so* kind."

"Simon's paying for this?" I said.

"His insurance," she said. The nurse came and directed me back to my room. Mom stayed through dinner. I could tell Elliot was waiting for her to leave. When she did, and the next bed was empty, he came out with it.

"We have things to discuss," he said.

"The cops want to talk to me," I said.

Elliot blinked. "How did you know?"

"Carl Williams escaped from prison," I said.

He stared at me. "Who told you?"

I gazed up at the ceiling. Crows were flocking on the hospital lawn. A car was coming up the driveway, two guys in the front seat. "When am I going home?" I said.

"Couple more days. Maybe sooner. How did you know about Carl Williams?"

The car swung past the lawn and the crows flapped shrieking into the trees. "I was listening," I said.

He looked at me oddly. "When they came to the house?"

I shook my head. "In the hospital."

"Denton, that's not possible, you were asleep. When the cops came to the house, you must have been eavesdropping. You just don't remember."

I wasn't in a mood to argue. "Yeah, whatever."

"I want to hear about this guy," said Elliot.

"Carl Williams? He's the one who looked after me in prison," I said. "He offered to help me escape if I didn't make parole."

"I see," said Elliot. "Well, they think he may have robbed Gwen Lefcourt's store."

"Do they," I said. In return for what?

"Would you know anything about that?" he said.

"No," I said. "I haven't spoken to Carl Williams. Not since I left prison."

"That's what I told them," said Elliot. He glanced

toward the corridor, lowering his voice. "Tell me, was this a big love affair or what?"

A nurse was in the doorway. "I wouldn't call it that, no," I said—the nurse was signaling for Elliot. He followed her down the hall, and I buzzed the aide for a phone. I called Fay's Big & Tall—Bettina, the Eskimo salesgirl, answered. Gwen was in New York, on a buying trip.

"This is Denton Hake, I did some work at the store."

"Right, oh I'm sorry. Are you feeling better?"

"Much better, thank you. Just tell her I called, okay?" I rolled on my side and closed my eyes, floating over the cold gray floor toward the door. I could see myself lying there, the leaves shimmering outside the window, the empty bed in my room above the garage. Beyond, in a square of light, Mimi sat drinking tequila. She looked out the window, poured herself another glass, then opened the bottom sideboard drawer and put the bottle underneath the tablecloths. The drawer slammed and I opened my eyes. I reached for the phone again and dialed Randy.

"This is Randy Nelson. If it's an emergency, press one and I will be paged. Otherwise, please leave a message at the beep."

"Hi, this is Denton Hake. I'm due to leave the hospital tomorrow. Eager to resume. If you haven't given away my time, I'll see you Tuesday at our regular hour."

I hung up. The nurse came into the doorway.

"You have visitors," she said.

Behind her were the cop with the beet-shaped skull, and his partner, Officer Potato Head. The nurse went away and they eased into the room, introducing themselves—Fremont and Burke.

"You up to answering some questions?" said Fremont.

"I'll try," I said.

"How's your memory these days?"

I watched them both. "Fine," I said.

"After a concussion," said Fremont, "people sometimes have problems."

"What did you want to ask me?" I said. Burke was taking out a little red notebook.

"You were out for several days," said Fremont. "Which they tell us is unusual."

"You weren't trying to avoid us, were you, Denton?"

"No, sir," I said.

"What can you tell us about Carl Williams?"

"Nothing you don't know," I said.

"Has Carl Williams tried to contact you?" said Burke.

"No," I said.

"You work for Simon Lefcourt, don't you?"

"Yes, thanks to Carl."

Burke scribbled away. "You know Lefcourt's daughter?" said Fremont.

"I've met her, yes."

"Spend any time with her?"

"We had lunch together," I said. "We were at a party. I did some work at her store."

"You know there was a robbery at her store?"

"Yes," I said.

"Can you help us out with that?"

I shook my head slowly. "Sorry."

"You remember what night that was?"

"Yes," I said. "I found out about it the next day."

"And where were you that night?" said Fremont.

Where indeed? My memory of that night was clear—I was watching Richard Nesbit grab Gwen by the hair. "Oaktree Estates."

"Can anyone confirm that?"

"Yes. Gwen Lefcourt."

Fremont shared a book with Burke—I gathered she'd already said as much. "Do you mind if we put a tap and trace on your phone?" Fremont said.

I shrugged. "It's not my phone. My brother pays the bill."

Burke closed his pad. "Thank you, Denton," said Fremont. They went out into the hall and I closed my eyes again, drifting with the crows through a cloudless sky. Below, Randy Nelson was getting out of a blue Honda, book bag slung over her shoulder. In her apartment there were clothes everywhere, dirty dishes, newspapers, takeout cartons. On the coffee table was a copy of *Penthouse*, on the toilet tank was a pile of *Playboys*. I saw her get up, go to the living room window, peer out, then draw the shades. She was crying. I felt somebody shake my shoulder.

"Denton?"

I opened my eyes.

"Doctor wants to ask some questions. Then we can go."

The doctor with the goatee came in, followed by a nurse and a couple of students.

"What did you have for breakfast, Denton?"

I looked at them all. "I didn't have breakfast this morning."

Apparently that was the right answer. The doctor pointed at one of the students, a girl with corkscrew curls. "Mr. Hake," she said, "can you tell me what this means? 'A friend in need is a friend indeed.' "

"That depends," I said.

"On what?" said the girl.

"It could mean, the best friends to have are the ones in trouble, because they really appreciate friendship. Usually, it means, when you're in trouble, that's when you find out who your friends are." I was thinking of Carl—I smiled at Elliot, then went on. "If that's two words, 'in deed,' then it could mean something else again."

The doctor nodded, then smacked a tuning fork against the bed and held it to my ankle bone. "Do you feel this?"

"Yes," I said. He tickled the soles of my feet. "I take it my CAT-scan was okay," I said.

"Perfectly normal," he said. They took turns shining a light in my eyes, and then they all filed out. The nurse returned with a form to sign, and she and Elliot wheeled me into the elevator and out into the lobby. Mom was waiting at the curb, at the wheel of a red Camaro.

"Happy Birthday," she said.

I'd been asleep for my birthday—totally ignored it. Then as Mom climbed out I realized what she meant—the car was for me.

"What did this set you back?" I asked Elliot.

"The insurance," said Elliot, starting behind the wheel.

"I'll drive," I said. I saw them trade looks, but nobody stopped me. I pulled out into traffic, feeling like a kid in Driver's Ed; the road fanning out like a video game. After a few blocks I got my bearings.

"What did the cops say to *you*?" I asked Elliot.

"Nothing." He shot me a cold look, meaning we weren't to discuss this in front of Mom. When we got to Elliot's, Mimi was in the kitchen—the dog licked my hand but Mimi wouldn't look at me, just went on browning the onions. Elliot suggested I take a nap before dinner—apparently the doctors had given him instructions. I didn't object, I felt a headache coming on, so I went on out to the garage and up to my room.

Everything looked different, everything looked the same. I lay down, facing the wall.

The plaster was faintly streaked with red.

At first I didn't understand, and then I looked at my knuckles—the scabs were almost healed. I must have flailed out in my sleep, watching Richard Nesbit threaten Gwen and grab her hair—but if all that time I was in bed, throwing ghost punches at the wall, how come I didn't see those bloodstains before? Because, I thought, you're such a guilty motherfucker—I could hear Carl Williams saying this. My headache eased and I dropped off to sleep, hoping to see Randy again, but all I saw when I opened my eyes was the ceiling of my bedroom, where several spider webs had formed in my absence. I closed my eyes again, and there I was in the dining room, watching Elliot explain to Mom about Carl.

I got out of bed, washed my face and went down to the house. They were three-quarters through dinner. I helped myself to soup.

"—reason we don't want blacks here," Mimi was saying, "has nothing to do with racism. White neighborhoods don't get robbed till black people move in."

I sat down in my chair. "Where did you read that?" I said.

"And you know why?" Elliot said. "Because inner-city blacks target suburban blacks. Black-on-black crime, I can show you the statistics."

"By the way," I said to Elliot, blowing on my

soup, "I never thanked you for the music. Who was that singer I didn't recognize?"

Elliot blinked at me. "Bonnie Raitt?"

"Oh, was that Bonnie Raitt? She sounded African."

Everybody fell silent. They left me alone to finish my dinner. Afterwards I walked Mom to her car.

"Are you all right?" she said.

"Never better," I said. And I grinned at her.

"You seem very up. Vicodin, is that what they gave you? I had that when I broke my hip." She paused before getting into her Riviera—there were some things she wanted to clear up. "They said your body ran hot and cold. They couldn't make head or tail of it."

"That's because I wasn't there."

"I'm sorry?"

"In my body."

She scrunched up her face—this was more than she wanted to hear, so I took it back. "I'm kidding," I said. "No, they didn't give me Vicodin."

"And what's all this about Gwen Lefcourt's store?"

"Somebody robbed it. She collected the insurance."

"And now she can pay her bills, that's what Elliot told me. Denny, just tell me you weren't involved."

"Well," I said, "you did raise your sons to be Good Samaritans."

"Denton," she said sharply.

"I'm joking, Mom."

"I know you're joking. Which means you had nothing to do with it. I'm sorry I asked." We kissed goodbye and I doubled back through the house. Elliot was washing up. Mimi was in the bedroom, watching TV with the door closed.

"Your wife's getting paranoid again," I said.

"Can you blame her? It's not every day the cops come to visit."

I thought maybe I wouldn't tell him, but then I did. "And she's still drinking," I said.

He stared at me. "What?" he said.

"Check the tablecloth drawer," I said. He didn't get up to look, and I didn't press it. I gave him a pat on the shoulder and headed out across the driveway to the garage. After a moment the back door banged open and Elliot came trotting across the lawn after me.

"How long has this been going on? When did you see her put the bottle there?"

"The other day," I said.

"What do you mean, the other day?"

"I'm tired, Elliot. I feel like I've been through a war. Can we talk about this tomorrow?" And I went up the stairs to my room. Out the window I could see him pacing, looking up at my window, trying to decide whether to bother me again. After a minute or so he went back to the house—I stripped off my clothes, took a pain pill and got into bed, staring up through the ceiling at the moon. I rolled over on my stomach and there they were below me, Mimi in bed, her arms folded, Elliot reading her the riot act.

"—Well, I've had it too. I can't take it anymore. You know he robbed her store—"

"Mimi, we don't know any such thing. The police are looking for Carl Williams, they questioned Gwen Lefcourt, she said Denny was somewhere in Oaktree Estates—"

"How does she know that?"

"He was following her. He was worried about her."

"Worried about her why? She's lying. They're in it together. If he didn't rob the store, why did he run away that night? What were those scabs on his knuckles?"

"I don't know. I don't think he knows."

"If he wants to destroy himself, why doesn't he just do it? Why doesn't he just shoot himself?"

I saw Elliot's hand go up, saw it before she did. She covered her face, too late to deflect the blow, and he fell into an armchair. For a long time they sat there like tiny statues, Mimi in bed, Elliot in the chair, the TV muted and playing over their faces.

"You're just blaming him. It's you. It's your lack of discipline."

"Shut up, Elliot."

She curled into fetal position.

"I wasn't brought up to live like this," she said. "This is not my life. Elliot, it's him or me."

The TV went off, the room went black. I could hear Mimi whimpering softly in the darkness. Elliot was just sitting there, and me, I was back in Mom's house, thinking about the time we heard moans coming from the master bedroom, only Elliot said that was Dot in there with Dad, not Mom, and as a child I wondered how could that be? The week before I'd seen Mom and Dad together in the backyard hammock, swaying slowly beneath the moon—didn't that mean they were in love? The memory faded, and then I saw Elliot get up and take a blanket out of the linen closet and clear the Presidential pillows from the living room couch. Mimi by now was snoring in the bedroom. I watched Elliot toss and turn on the couch for a while. Then I slid my hand under the pillow and fell asleep.

9

And where were you?"

I was watching two raindrops wriggle down Randy's windowpane. "I was looking down on the bed," I said.

"From where?"

"I don't know. From up high. From the corner of the room."

"Moving?"

"Yeah," I said. "Was I moving, you mean? Yes."

"What, like bouncing along the ceiling? Like a balloon?"

I sighed. "Fuck you," I said.

Randy sat there in silence for a while.

"Hey," I said, "I can keep this up as long as you can."

She didn't say anything. We both watched the rain.

"Your parole's almost up," she said at last.

"I know," I said. "Ortega's caseload got too heavy." I checked out her reaction—deadpan. "You think that's wrong, don't you? You think I oughta be locked up, you and my sister-in-law, you're two peas in a pod. I'm sorry," I said suddenly. "It's happening right now, okay? I can get up out of this chair and walk right out the door. And I'd still be here watching you walk around your office, talking on the phone."

"Sounds like fun," she said dryly.

"It is," I said. "It's like a flying dream. Except you're really going someplace."

"Last time you were here you couldn't do that."

"I could do it. I just didn't know what I was doing."

"So the accident jarred something loose."

"It woke me up," I said. "It made everything more intense. Doesn't head trauma do that sometimes?"

She didn't answer, and that told me I was pissing in the wind. "Where were you going the night of the accident? Who were you running from?"

So Elliot had clued her in. "The police." I rubbed my knuckles. "They came to the house. I thought maybe I'm nuts, maybe I did rob Gwen's store. Then in the hospital I heard who they were looking for—Carl Williams."

"You think he might have done the robbery?"

Don't go there, I thought. "I have no idea," I said. I leaned forward suddenly. "Who's the guy who ditched you?" I said.

I saw Randy's cheek twitch. "I'm sorry, what?"

"I saw you in your apartment," I said. "You were wiping away tears. You looked up, you realized somebody was looking, you went over to the window, you closed the shutters."

She shook her head no. "My apartment doesn't have shutters."

"The shades," I said. "Your place is a mess, by the way."

She blinked. "Who else have you visited?"

I shrugged. "Mimi. Elliot."

"Gwen?" she said.

"No," I said. "I don't know."

"The night of the robbery? Didn't you say you were looking in Richard Nesbit's window?"

My head was starting to hurt. "I don't know where Gwen is. She's been out of town. New York."

"And you can't picture that? Why, too far away? Never been there? You didn't know where *I* lived, did you? Or maybe you looked that up in the phone book."

"No," I said, puzzled. "I didn't."

"Why not?" she said. "Most patients do." She put on a gentle smile. "You see what I'm saying, Denton?"

"Yes. You think I came to your place, I spied in your window and I don't remember, I'm a Peeping Tom and I won't admit it to myself. You know what? If my parole's up, then I don't have to come here anymore, right?"

"How can you see without eyes? What does the seeing? What absorbs the light?"

"It doesn't work that way," I said. "I don't know. You *are* the light."

"And meanwhile your body goes on functioning. Walking, talking, seeing what *it* sees—"

"Yes. I know you think that's impossible—"

She smiled patiently. "Denton, they've tried to do studies on remote viewing—"

"Nothing remote about it. I'm *there*. Jesus," I said. "Okay, you're right. I'm crazy. I do things and I dream about them later. I peeked in Richard Nesbit's window, saw him beating up on Gwen, and then came back and socked my bedroom wall. Right, and

I didn't see those *Playboys* in your bathroom. Which doesn't have a window, as I recall.''

She looked at me hard. ''And I don't have a boyfriend.''

''Girlfriend, then.''

She shut up like a clam.

''Is that just a lucky guess? Is that what you're gonna tell me?''

Yes, I'd hit a nerve. ''I'd like to hypnotize you now,'' she said quietly.

''You gonna ask me if I robbed Gwen's store?''

''Not if you don't want me to.''

''Because I didn't. Any more than I raped Sandra Loyacano. I had sex with her. It was voluntary.''

''Okay,'' she said.

''In the pool, on the floor, in her mother's bed, why are you looking at me like that, it's true! You helped me remember!''

''Denton, I believe you—''

''She was living in her mom's house, she wasn't supposed to let anybody in, so when her mom came home and found stuff missing, she lied and said she was raped—''

Randy held up a hand. ''We can go into all this later. Can you close your eyes now, please?''

''She made it up, you understand what I'm saying, that little cockteaser? There wasn't any assault, all I did was take some money, six months on highway cleanup instead of four years of hell, that *cunt*—oh Jesus—''

''Denton!''

She said it so sharply I weakened. I heard myself say, ''All right.''

Damn, I thought. She was on me before I could change my mind.

"I want you to imagine a hundred candles, and I want you to blow them out one by one—"

"Aw shit," I said, but suddenly there was Gwen, fluffing her lemon-yellow hairdo, coming out of a bathroom—her bathroom, not a hotel room. She was here, she was in town. "She's back," I said.

"It's okay. Take it easy. You know you're here with me, because you can feel my hand, right?"

There was someone in Gwen's bed. Gwen was parading along the side, naked, just out of reach.

"I'd like you to picture the house you grew up in."

It was so dark I couldn't see, slivers of daylight seeping through where the curtains were drawn, curtains that matched the canopy over Gwen's bed. Was Nesbit's gold Lexus outside, I wondered, and then I saw a hand reach out and pull her onto the bed.

"I'd like you to think back to a time your father was alive."

The hand was black against her back, the nails were pink.

"She's with somebody," I said.

Black hands, pink nails. He was fondling her breasts. Music was playing, something New Age, massage music.

"Do you remember the day your father died?"

"No," I said.

"Start as far back as you can. Try and tell a story, don't worry if you can't remember details—"

"I don't want to do this anymore," I said. I opened my eyes. "I really don't," I said.

"What are you seeing?"

"Gwen," I said.

"What is she doing?"

"She's naked. I can't see her anymore." I rubbed my eyes. "She was having sex."

"With who?"

It was gone. All I could see now was Sandra Loyacano's house.

"You remember what we were talking about?"

I was back in her parents' bedroom, giving Sandra Loyacano head on the green shag carpet. "Yeah," I said. "You were grilling me about my dad."

"Grilling you?"

Refocusing, I looked at my watch. "Yeah, exactly like a cop."

"Is that why you stopped?"

"No. I don't know. Anyhow, your next patient's here," I said.

She shook her head. "My next hour's open," she said.

"Then he came at the wrong time. Check it out, he looks like Pinocchio," I said. It was true, I could picture him in the lobby, a needle-nosed guy in a black vest and orange shirt. Randy got up and looked out the window. The patient's car was there—it showed in her face.

"Well?" I said.

She was trying to get a grip. Suddenly I felt bad for her.

"It's okay," I said. "We'll try that again on Friday. See you in my dreams," I added, just to rub it in. I walked out of her office and down to the lobby, past the patient with the long skinny nose. What did I care if she believed me? This time I'm not coming back, I thought, slamming the car door. For a minute I sat there, like I was expecting Randy to come and drag me back inside—then I was out on the highway, the Camaro was driving itself, and there was Gwen, pumping away in her bedroom, right behind my eyes.

I pulled over to the side of the road.

Stop torturing yourself, I thought, it's Sandra Loy-acano you're pissed at, not Gwen. There's nobody in Gwen's bed, Carl isn't fucking her, you're letting your anger play tricks on you. Carl wouldn't do that to his friend.

You wish.

Randy's right, you don't want to know. You're a coward, I thought.

I got back on the road. I drove to Gwen's house—the Camaro drove me. There was no car outside, so I got out and looked through the bars of her garage. No sign of her Cherokee, no sign of Carl—I got back in my car. I drove to Renton, barely feeling my hands on the wheel, and parked in the alley behind the mini-mall. The glass in her back window had been re-placed—there was still a sticker on it—and the Cherokee was parked near the back door. Gwen was with a customer. When I walked in, a look came over her face—more surprised than happy, I thought. She steered the customer to Bettina, hurried over to me. I pulled her into the office, gave her a kiss.

"What are you—"

I kissed her neck, I inhaled her. She smelled of soap and perfume.

"How was New York?"

"New York was great. I tried to call you, you're not listed. Then I called your brother, but he hung up on me. Why didn't you tell me you were coming?"

I kicked the door closed. She kissed me hard. I lifted up her sweater and undid her bra.

"Wait," she said.

"I hear the insurance money came through," I said.

"Denton, this is crazy—"

She slid the bolt lock on the office door. I kissed her nipples. "How much did you get?" I said.

"Stop." I had my hand between her legs. "We are not going to talk about this. Ever."

"Thanks for the alibi, by the way."

"But you *had* an alibi," she said. Her voice was growing thick. "You followed me to Richard's."

I kissed her on the mouth. "Who robbed the store?"

"Shh," she said, nodding toward the door.

"Who was at your place this afternoon?"

"Where?"

"Your condo. Are you seeing Carl Williams?"

Instead of answering me she kissed me.

"Are you sleeping with Carl?"

"Oh God," she said. My hand was between her legs. "Denny, I missed you," and she eased down to my crotch. She laid her tongue along the underside of my cock, then held it and started to suck hard. I started to drift up, beyond the walls, beyond the ceiling. The gold Lexus was pulling into the lot. I raised up, looked at her. We were on the floor.

"It's Richard."

"No," she said. Her legs were around me. "What are you talking about."

"He's almost here." I was inside her. "Hurry up."

"No. I can't."

"He's coming up the sidewalk."

"Don't tease. Don't stop."

There was a knock on the office door. We both heard Bettina's voice. "Gwen, Richard's here."

She was starting to come. Bettina knocked again. "Gwen?"

She shuddered, half with pleasure, half with fright. "Tell him I'll be right out. Oh Jesus," she said softly. I helped her button up, pulled up my pants, zipped up. She waited at the office door while I slipped out the back—I jumped in my Camaro and started it up, down the alley and around to the front. Richard Nesbit's Lexus was parked near the store. I tried to see in, make sure he wasn't hassling her again, and he wasn't, not in front of Bettina and the other salesgirl—then Richard came out the front door in a hurry, Gwen behind him, calling to him, but he didn't stop, he got right back in his Lexus. Gwen went back inside the store. I eased the Camaro out of the space and onto the highway.

I drove straight to work. I couldn't get out of my head, I was too wrought-up—I pictured Gwen talking to customers, but that was only an idea, and I couldn't picture Richard Nesbit at all. When I got to the job site Boris took me aside, asked me how I was feeling. I told him I was fine—which was a lie, I had a headache coming on—and he put me to work tightening screws on the shelving. It was dull work, and suddenly I wasn't doing it. I was drifting over a carnival site, out on Route 99, listening to the screams from the Tilt-a-Whirl, as if I expected to see Gwen in one of the buckets, checking out an interracial couple on the midway, but no sign of Carl either, thinking, no, you're just playing hooky, and with that I was back at the job site, sorting through a hand of draw poker. All the shelves were done. I'd had a productive morning, everybody seemed glad to have me back, nobody was saying anything about my accident—apparently it wasn't common knowledge.

Hard as I tried, all I could see of Gwen was a blur, though I could still smell her on my fingers. I was up a few dollars when Simon's Caddy pulled into the lot.

Nesbit's Lexus was right behind him.

They huddled in the shed all afternoon—I could see them in there, arguing over blueprints. About three o'clock I began to tire. Boris saw this, and told me to go home, but as I started for my car I saw Richard come up behind me. Even before I turned I knew he was in a wild frame of mind.

"Where you going, Hake? Come back here."

I didn't speed up, I didn't slow down.

"Hake. That's a kind of fish, isn't it? Were you named for a fish? Denton Cod."

"Why don't you try and chill," I said.

Suddenly he said, "I'm sorry."

I was about to get in the Camaro. I stared at him, wondering if he had a pistol in his waistband.

"You don't know what you're dealing with here," he said.

I played dumb. "Dealing with where?"

"You know what I'm talking about. Gwenny-poo."

He grinned a weird grin, laughing through his teeth. He's drunk, I thought.

"Our Gwen would fuck a snake. In fact, she is fucking a snake. A blacksnake, to be precise."

Something cold washed over me. "Just take it easy," I heard myself say, like I was saying it to myself.

"And she's getting weirder. I almost caught her this afternoon. She was doing him in her store, can you believe that?"

Yes, there was liquor on his breath. "No, frankly,

I can't," I said. I unlocked the Camaro.

"What kind of gun does he favor, would you know?"

"We never discussed it."

"Carl's the reason I got into guns, you know."

"No, I didn't know," I said. I got behind the wheel and he bellied up to the door.

"You couldn't get me a nine, could you?"

"A what?" I said.

"A nine millimeter pistol, isn't that a nigger gun? I bet that's what he's into."

He was toying with my side mirror. Steady, I told myself—you go off on him now, he's going to take it out on Gwen again.

"Richard," I said, starting the Camaro, "I really think you oughta try and sober up."

"Don't stiff me, Hake, I've had a bad week. What do you say, I'll buy you a drink. They let you guys drink, don't they? Isn't your parole about up?"

I took his hand by the wrist and removed it from my car. "Stay away from Gwen," I warned him, and eased away toward the gate. In the rearview I saw him cup his hands and yell something at me—I kept right on going, heading back to Elliot's. I couldn't stop thinking about Carl, his hand on Gwen's back, the New Age music playing on her bedroom stereo. Of course Gwen had slept with Carl, I'd seen that in her face, that first lunch by the lake. My heart kept sinking—I prayed God to let me alone, deliver me from this confusion or just let me go peacefully nuts. Then I started to think of something Mom used to say, about how God doesn't listen to self-pity, even if it's couched as prayer, how you can't fool Him, especially when He's fucking with you. I should be praying for guidance and self-mastery. God had given me a gift, and it was up to me to use it properly. Then I realized this *was* the prayer, and this lightness in my heart was God's answer, or so Mom would say.

I drove home.

Mimi's car wasn't in the driveway—Elliot was in the kitchen, making us both something for dinner.

I started up the driveway toward the garage. As I took out my key I heard twigs crackling—I swung around wildly, bracing myself.

"Ozzie?" I said—what I was really thinking was Nesbit. But there was nobody. I started to open the door and then I heard her voice.

"Denny?"

It was Gwen. The brush crackled again and she came slinking around the corner of the garage, in a pale blue belly shirt, hair wet, looking frightened—both of us did.

"I didn't see your car," I said.

"I parked it around the corner." She knew to avoid Elliot, though I wasn't sure why—I followed her up the stairs, closed the door behind us.

"You want a drink? I can get something from the house."

She shook her head. She was already buzzed, or maybe it was just fear. "I gave Richard back his ring," she said.

"Whoa," I said. "You picked a bad day."

"*My* ring. He couldn't even choose a ring, he had to ask my advice. He's a total mental leech, I don't know what I ever saw in him."

"And how did he react?" I asked. As if I didn't know.

"If it wasn't for my father, he wouldn't have a single client."

''Did he threaten you again?''

''That's just it. He was cool as ice. It was so scary. Denny, I'm sorry, you've risked your life for me already—''

''Have I? How?''

''At the party. Coming home with me that night. Following me to his house—you don't know how nuts he is—''

''Did he have a gun today?''

''He *always* has a gun.'' She sank down on the couch. ''I think about you all the time,'' she said.

I sat down next to her. ''Even when you were with Carl?''

For a second it was like I'd said something in Chinese. ''You're so good and I'm so horrible,'' she said, and started to cry. Her shoulders shook. Suddenly I was outside my window, looking in—I had my arm around her, holding her close, trying to calm her. Below, I saw Elliot walking across the lawn toward the garage.

''Denny?'' he called. ''Dinner's ready.''

I saw my face in the window, heard myself call back down. ''Be right there,'' I said, but Elliot was already coming up the stairs.

I hustled Gwen into the bedroom, shut the door.

The stairway door opened. He can smell her, I was thinking—his eyes were darting around. ''Mimi here yet?'' I said.

''No,'' he said. ''No no no.''

''Where'd she go?''

He shook his head vaguely. ''I could use a drink before dinner, you got anything to drink?''

''No,'' I said. He was looking right at the bedroom door. ''I don't keep anything up here.''

''You sure?'' he said.

"Yes, I'm sure," I said.

He backed away from the bedroom door. "Mimi's big suitcase is gone," he said, and suddenly fell to one knee. I couldn't make sense of what he was doing—he shoved an armchair out of the way and socked the floor. One of the floorboards leaped up—under it was a bottle of brandy. "See, you were wrong," he said, lifting the bottle out. "Can you believe Mimi'd go to this trouble?" He unscrewed the cork, sniffed the brandy. "She used to sleep up here when I was snoring every night."

"Elliot, it doesn't mean she's left you," I said, watching him rinse out my toothbrush glass. He bolted two fingers of brandy and offered me the bottle—I took a courtesy nip and handed it back. For a minute he just stared into space—then he took a step back into the main room, and spun around again. I thought maybe he'd heard Mimi's car pull into the driveway, but then he stopped outside the bedroom door, glaring at it. That's when I realized Gwen's bag had been sitting there the whole time.

He pushed open the door—I heard Gwen squeal with fright.

"Jesus," I said.

He backed out of the bedroom. Gwen came tiptoeing into the main room. "I'm going," she said.

"Gwen, this is my brother Elliot—"

"We met at the hospital," said Elliot. From above I saw the three of us, Elliot turning away sharply, as though staring at her would turn his body to stone, Gwen backing toward the stairway door, me picking up her bag and handing it to her.

"I'll call you," she said. At that Elliot spun around again—they started jawing at each other and I was chiming in and the next thing I knew Gwen was going down the stairs as fast as her legs would carry her. I was right behind her, hovering at her shoulder as she hurried toward her Cherokee. The door slammed and there was Elliot in front of my eyes.

"—Didn't that accident teach you anything? You want to ruin what's left of your life? Who the hell is Richard Nesbit?"

"Guy she was engaged to," I said.

"I'm going to call your therapist."

"She's scared to death—Elliot? Give her a break."

"Listen to me." He had me by the arm. "Gwen Lefcourt isn't worth hellroom. I know all about the insurance hustle. Everybody knows. I called her insurance company, they know the claim was inflated, the jewelry was worthless, but they're not going to fight it, they don't have enough evidence."

I yanked my arm free. "Why is this your business?"

"*You* are my business. *You*." He was looking out the window toward the house. Suddenly I guessed it.

"You told Mimi about the liquor bottle, didn't you?"

"What are you talking about?"

"In the tablecloth drawer. You confronted her. That's why she cleared out. You looked there and you found it."

He clicked his teeth together, held them together, like Mom in one of her moods.

"Elliot, I can't help what I see," I said. "It just happens. How did I know about Bonnie Raitt? How did I know there was *any* music? You can *ask* my therapist," I said. "I saw Randy Nelson crying, I saw *Playboys* in her bathroom, and there's no man in her life, okay? At least I'm starting to control it.''

''What does she say when you talk like this?''

''Randy? She listens. She wonders. Sometimes she believes me.''

''Denny, for Christ's sake. We've gotta find you a real doctor.''

''No, you don't,'' I said calmly. ''Listen, I'm sorry I said anything about Mimi. Next time I'll keep it to myself.''

He hung his head. His eyes were closed. In the other room, the phone rang.

''Don't answer it,'' he said. He stomped the loose floorboard back into place.

''Maybe it's your wife,'' I said.

''She wouldn't call me up here. It's probably Gwen Lefcourt calling from her car. I said don't answer,'' he said. He grabbed me like he was about to hit me, then sat down on the window seat, drumming his fist on his knee. The phone was still ringing. I was trying to picture Gwen, but all I could make out was the lights of her Cherokee racing through the trees.

''She's scared,'' I said. ''She's asking for my help, you can understand that, can't you?''

I picked up the phone.

''Denton?'' said a man's voice.

''Tell her you're not coming over,'' said Elliot. He stood up again.

''Hello, who is this?'' I said into the phone.

''How quickly they forget,'' said the man's voice.

My eyes closed. For an instant I saw my dad's bloody face.

''Come on, no bullshit, Denny, I need you. Don't trip out on me, okay? Hello? Come on, baby, I know you're there. Denny?''

10

I'm sorry, who do you want?''

On the other end, I heard Carl Williams light a cigarette and blow out smoke.

"Take down this number," he said.

Elliot was standing right next to me. "This is not a good time," I said.

"674-6728. Did you get that?"

I said the number to myself in my head. "Some other time."

"I *said*, can you remember that?"

"Yes," I said. "I heard you."

"I'm counting on you, Denny."

"Goodbye," I said. I hung up. My heart was somewhere near my shoes.

"Who was that?" asked Elliot.

"Political call."

"The hell it was."

"If you don't mind, I'd like to go to sleep now."

"I want to talk about Gwen Lefcourt. I want to talk about why she was thrown out of school."

"I don't know anything about it," I said. The phone number was fading in my mind. 67, 67, four times two is eight. 674-6728.

"Sexual misconduct," he said.

"Whatever that means. I don't care what you think, Gwen Lefcourt is not the Devil. Can we talk about this tomorrow?"

"You're gonna spend the night with her, aren't you?"

I had to get him out of there. "I may move in with her," I said.

"Oh Jesus, Denny."

"Forget it. I'm going to bed, okay? I'm not going anywhere, I've got a headache."

He just stood there.

"Suit yourself," I said. I squeezed past him and into the bedroom, pretending to undress for bed. A couple of minutes later I heard him go back down the stairs, saw him disappear into the house. My head was still reeling—I found a pen, wrote the phone number Carl had given me on my wrist, then turned off the lights and drew the shades.

For several minutes I stood at the window. Elliot was somewhere in the house, lying facedown—in the living room, on the couch, face buried in Abraham Lincoln's. The floor tilted below me and I floated toward the window above the garage. There was no one in my room—I was gone, I was out the door, tearing down the stairs and up the driveway to my car.

"Denton!" I heard Elliot cry.

I was too far ahead of him—no way he could get to his car in time to follow. First the Camaro was below me and then I was behind the wheel, pulling into a mall I didn't recognize. What was I doing here? I got out of the car, went into a video arcade, asked for the phone. Like an idiot I stood there watching myself dial and redial—finally I let the phone ring on the other end. One ring was all it took.

"Okay," said Carl, as if he'd been watching me, too. "Now give me the number there and I'll call you back."

He was taking no chances. Two minutes later the pay phone rang.

"Now it's just me and you," he said. "How are you?"

"I'm all right," I said.

"You had an accident."

"Yeah," I said. "Who told you?"

He let that go without answering. "Does your head still leak?"

"It's worse and it's better," I said.

"The St. Regis," he said. "North of Pioneer Square, about ten blocks. You know where that is?"

"Yeah, the Regis, I can find it."

"Denny, I need start-up money. Got to buy a passport."

Some kids were standing behind me, waiting to use the phone. "What's the matter, couldn't Gwen help you out?"

His silence was like a kick in the gut. "Would I be calling you?" he said.

"I guess not," was all I said.

"Can you be here by eleven? Are you near an ATM?"

I was trying to picture Richard Nesbit, but I couldn't see him. "Yeah, I can try to be there by eleven."

"Okay. Denny, you're a prince."

"I can only get three hundred," I said. "That's all I can withdraw per day."

"Every little bit helps. I missed you, Denton. Crazy motherfucker."

"Yeah, well," I said lamely, and hung up without

saying goodbye. I went out the back door and around to my Camaro. Nobody followed me out of the lot—I drove around the block once, just to make sure, then back through Renton till I came to an ATM machine. Nobody was there, nobody was watching. I took out $300, then went into the all-night grocery, bought some doughnuts and milk for Carl, paid with my ATM card and asked for $100 over. The clerk gave me two fifties and a long look. I got back in my car and started for downtown, fixing my eyes on the car ahead, glancing regularly in the rearview. I could hear voices in my head, a woman's voice, a toilet flushing, something that sounded like Carl grunting, but the line of brake lights in front of me was all I saw. I got off at the exit, did a figure-eight around a couple of blocks—nobody behind me, so I drove past the square to the St. Regis Hotel. There were a dozen lights on six or seven floors, a couple of homeless people in the alley, and what looked like a pair of hookers coming along the sidewalk. One of them was walking toward my car—I saw her go up to the passenger seat window, glance in, then walk on by. That's when I realized the Camaro was empty.

Shit, I thought.

My car was somewhere below me, across from the Regis, no one at the wheel.

Jesus, I thought. Then suddenly the street was gone. Carl was shaking his finger in my face.

"—Where are you?"

He pulled me close, searching me with his blood-shot eyes. Across the hotel room a red-haired woman with a nose-ring was watching TV.

"Mona," said Carl, "he's tripping out again."

"No," I said. "I'm listening." I rolled a finger and thumb into my eyes. "So how *did* you get out?"

His shoulders slumped. "You just asked me that."

"The laundry truck?" I said.

"What the fuck is wrong with you? Are you with us or not?"

"I'm here," I insisted. The red-haired woman, Mona, was smack up against the screen, turning the channels by hand. The room smelled of vomit—then I saw pizza cartons on the bed.

"I ain't got time," he said, "to be doing nobody no favors."

"Favors," I heard myself say. Whatever this was about, he was lying, I could tell from the way he turned his back on me.

"Insurance scams. I leave that to folks like you. I'm the kind of man, freedom makes me nervous, I gotta pick my spots in case I get tempted to fuck up."

It popped out. "You have time to fuck Gwen, though."

For a second he didn't say anything. I was hoping against hope he'd prove me wrong.

"Gwen's boyfriend saw you," I said.

"Gwen's boyfriend. I thought *you* were her boyfriend."

"Yeah, so did I." I was trying to picture Gwen, see if Nesbit's Lexus was anywhere on her block, but Carl was in my face.

"Are you carrying a gun?"

I oughta be, I thought. "No," I said.

"Don't get touchy, I'm just asking." He shot a glance at Mona, lowering his voice for her benefit. "Think about it, Denton. Would I be caught dead around that girl's house?"

"Why not? You've been locked up a long time."

That seemed to silence him. He started to shake his head, slowly, side to side. "Mona, go downstairs and get us a bottle of—what do you like, scotch?"

He was talking to me. "Sure," I said. Mona looked at the twenty in Carl's hand—a crumpled one, not one of the ATM bills. She took it and went out the door. Carl waited at the window until she was out of the building, while I checked my wallet—the $300 from the ATM and the $100 from the convenience store were still there. Carl sat down on the bed.

"Okay, you want to hear about it? Or you want to keep torturing yourself."

I looked at my watch. Gwen was certainly home by now.

"She asked me to rob her store. She wasn't sure you were down for the cause."

"So you obliged her," I said.

He shrugged. "We used to be an item."

"Yes, I know."

"*Used* to be," he insisted.

I wanted to believe him. "So how much did you get?"

"Me? I didn't even get the register, okay? Nobody got hurt, except maybe the insurance company, and they'll raise her rates, so it all evens out in the end. I just brokered a loan from the insurers."

"Yeah, you're a saint," I said.

"Denton, what is your *problem*."

"What were you doing there—" I tried to remember the day, "—Tuesday afternoon?"

His eyes widened. He grunted. "That was *you* outside?"

"Why, who'd you think it was?"

"Mr. Gold Lexus. Mr. Firing Range." He rose and went into the bathroom. After a while I heard the toilet flush, and then a key turned in the front door—I was so wired I bolted up from the chair. It was Mona, back with the bottle of scotch. Carl came out of the bathroom, saw me standing there frozen.

"You okay?" he said. "You're not going to pieces, are you?"

I sat down again. "Yes and no."

He laughed at that. "Well," he said, "you're facing some facts about yourself."

"I've been getting some therapy," I said, watching Mona unscrew the top off the bottle of scotch. Carl's hand was on my shoulder. I was thinking about Dad, trying to remember the sound of the gun when it went off the second time.

"All that suicide shit you couldn't remember."

"It's coming back," I said.

"You still traveling?"

"More than ever."

"Lemme feel your skin." He put his hand on my face, my throat. "Yeah, you're starting to feel cold. What's the matter, what's your hurry?"

I was looking at my watch. "Gwen," I said. My mouth was drying up. "She's in danger."

"Who, from you?" He laughed. "Who do you think you are, the motherfucking Lone Ranger?"

"Shut up," I said. I gripped my knees. I wanted to be anywhere but here, but here I was.

"Stay here. Don't be rushing off to Gwen." He patted my hand. "Mona," he said, "why don't you take Denton's mind for a walk, let me and his body have a quick one."

I started for the door, then realized I was still sitting there. Mona was pouring scotch into a 7-Up can. "You guys think you're so weird."

"I'm kidding," said Carl, reaching out for her hand. "You don't have to go down to the corner, you can watch."

"Pass," said Mona.

"Why not?"

Mona shrugged. "Doesn't interest me," she said. She turned up the volume on the TV, lay back on the bed. "I'll watch a man suck another man off," she said.

I started for the door again. "Good luck," I said to Carl.

"Butt-fucking, that's another story," said Mona.

"Oh, why's that another story?" asked Carl.

"That's like watching an operation on TV."

"Denton, where you going, man? I'm just fucking with you."

I was taking my wallet out of my pocket. The money was gone. Then I saw it in his hand.

"Listen to me. Listen to your only friend. I know people in Canada. You could join me in Vancouver, keep each other out of trouble, what do you think? I understand what you're going through, why do you think I came back to Seattle?"

"For the money."

"Cynical motherfucker. You need me and I need you."

"I've got to go," I heard myself say. My voice sounded a football field away.

"Forget Gwen, she'll only fuck you up more. Tell me what you're gonna do."

I was going. I was gone. I was running down the hall.

"Denton, come back!"

He came running toward me. I saw him stop at the stairwell, then turn around and go back inside the room. I followed him in. Mona was pouring him a drink.

"Motherfucker's crazy."

"What's his trip exactly?"

"You don't want to know. He's jealous. He's pissed off. I think he *is* carrying a gun."

"Did you fuck his girlfriend?"

"Yeah, I fucked the lady. She's nobody's girl-friend."

He flung himself on the bed. I looked around the room. Neon light was seeping in the window.

"How much money did he give you?"

I was nowhere in the room.

"Four hundred and change. Shit."

"Carl, where you going?"

"He's liable to do something. Stay here." I saw him bolt out the door and I flew toward the neon. Two homeless guys were scuffling below me on the corner. I looked up and down the street. My heart gave a sick lurch.

My Camaro was gone.

The earth tilted under me, the city with its lights rising up to meet my body, the moon racing above my head. The road was empty. All the crickets in the world were singing in my ears—suddenly there was Elliot's house below me, the two chimneys, the yard, the window over the garage.

The light was on.

I soared toward the light. The room spun. I looked for my bed in the darkness.

The bed was empty.

My body wasn't there.

Oh Jesus, I thought.

The walls tumbled around me. A surge of fear blew me back across the yard—a tree branch snapped in my head. That was the sound I was trying to re-member, the sound from the cellar the day Dad died, a mild little crack like something Dad was working on had broken, a chair leg, a table leg. I remembered us looking in the cellar window, the one Dad gated over after thieves had burglarized the house, me running in after Elliot with the football under my arm, down the cellar stairs. Then darkness sucked me back. Below me was a street, deserted, absolutely still.

It was Gwen's street.

Her condo was halfway up the block. Somebody was running out the door, man or woman I couldn't tell, into the street and around the corner. The ground raced beneath me. I was flying on pure fear, sputtering through the air like a pricked balloon, unable to make out the road, just the tops of the evergreens, the telephone wires, the car racing below, flashing between the tree trunks. I dived through the darkness, Elliot's house below me now and a car's headlights coming closer, blinding me. The car pulled to the curb.

I put it in park and got out.

A light went on across the street. "Blessings," I heard somebody say.

I jumped a foot. It was April Hartigan, the dog-walker. I glanced toward the house.

"What time is it?" I said.

She didn't even look at her watch. "It's eleven fifty-eight."

"What are you doing out here?" I heard myself say. I could see Elliot inside the house—Mimi was with him. Without waiting for an answer I started for the garage, softening my tread, past their bedroom window. Mimi was throwing clothes on the bed—the room was full of cartons. Elliot was pacing, talking in a low, angry voice—I couldn't make it out. As soon as I was past their window I ran for the garage and up the stairs, locking the door behind me.

I picked up the phone, dialed Gwen's number.

The phone rang once, twice, three times.

"Hi, this is you know who. Leave a message after the beep."

"Gwen," I heard myself say, "Pick up." I could see her lying there. The machine was in her living room, her bedroom ringer must be turned off—I hung up and tried again.

"Hi, this is you know who. Leave a message after the beep."

"Gwen! It's me, wake up!"

I sat down on my bed. The room went dark. She was lying there face up. I tried to see and saw my body rise up from the bed and walk out the door— by the time I caught up I was behind the wheel, heading east. I kept my eyes glued to the road, fixed on the white line. Trees filed past like soldiers. I was trying to see her face, her sleeping face, but all I could make out was the sawhorse at the bottom of her street.

I turned the corner.

Three Auburn police cars were parked in front of her condo.

I felt my heart die inside my chest.

I pulled over, got out of the car. People were drifting out of the neighboring condos.

I could see her inside, lying face up in her living room.

My knees weakened and I had to balance myself against a tree trunk. I coughed up stomach acid. A cop was stepping around her body to get up the stairs to the bedroom.

Blood was oozing into the carpet from a hole in her chest.

My mind went blank and I couldn't see her any-more. All I could picture was Dad lying on the cellar floor next to his tool bench, blood running from his face, the gun in his hand, which was still twitching. I started back toward my car. Running, not thinking, the way I'd run back up the cellar stairs after seeing Dad on the floor.

It wasn't until I got back behind the wheel that I realized who was watching me, and by then it was too late.

I turned off the ignition.

Two uniformed cops were trotting toward me across the lawn.

11

I got out of the Camaro.

My mind was buzzing and reeling, but I was still there. I knew how careful I had to be. I knew I had to stay inside myself—if ever I couldn't afford to leave myself behind, it was now. Beyond that, I don't know how much I understood.

"You want to step away from the car?" one of the uniforms said.

I complied. "What's happening?" I said.

"Can we see some ID?"

"Sure," I said. I started to reach for my wallet.

"Tell you what," said the cop. "Put your hands on the car and we'll get it."

"Make up your mind," I said—I heard that come out of my mouth, and I told myself to be calm. One of the cops took my wallet out of my pocket, patted me down—I was still babbling. "My name's Denton Hake, I came to see Gwen Lefcourt. She lives in that building, is she all right?" Hoping against hope—I couldn't shut myself up.

"You'd better come with us, Denton."

He handed me back my license while the other cop went inside Gwen's condo—I was close enough now to see through her window, the silhouettes moving

through her living room. I tried to see more but I
didn't dare let go—TV trucks were pulling up. Then
the second cop came out again, with a guy in street
clothes. A TV light came on—right away I recognized beet-head, Fremont, from the hospital.

"Detective Fremont?" I said. "I'm Denton
Hake."

"Yes, you are," he said. He motioned to somebody else, I couldn't see who. "What are you doing
here?"

"Has something happened to Gwen?"

He cocked his head—I saw razor burn on his neck.
"You were coming to see Gwen Lefcourt?"

"Yes, sir. Please, tell me what's going on."

"You're a friend of Gwen's."

"I told you that. A good friend." Otherwise, what
was I doing here at two a.m.? I felt sweat pop from
my scalp.

"Are you okay, Mr. Hake?"

Maybe if I left myself alone, I could stop sweating.
"This happens," I said, blotting my forehead,
"whenever I hear bad news."

"I haven't told you any news," said Fremont.

I don't have to be here, I thought. I can leave and
never come back.

"She's dead, isn't she?" I said.

Fremont said nothing. I felt my legs start to buc-
kle.

"I'm sorry, I have to sit down." The ground tilted,
but I was still here. I felt somebody's hand under my
elbow, and the next thing I knew I was sitting at the
curb—camera lights were swiveling in my direction,
one of the uniformed cops was shooing them back.

"We don't have to do this now," said Fremont,
taking out a pad.

"It's all right. I'm all right."

"When did you last see Gwen Lefcourt?"

I tried to think. The person leaving her condo, was that me, did I follow myself home? No, I told myself. It can't be. No way, you're not capable. Just hold onto that thought. "Not tonight," I said. "Is that what you mean?"

"The last time you saw her, when was that?"

My head spun as I tried to focus. "Earlier," I said.

"Earlier where?"

"At my place. My room. She came over." It was slowly coming back. "I promised to come see her later. That's why I'm here." I closed my eyes, trying to remember when else we'd talked. "I called her answering machine, I didn't get her."

"When? How long ago?"

For a second I couldn't remember. "As long as it took me to get over here," I said. "When she didn't answer, I got concerned."

He cocked his head. "Why did you get concerned?"

Steady, I told myself. "Because somebody was threatening to kill her."

"Somebody."

"Richard Nesbit. Her fiancé. She was terrified, she wanted me to spend the night."

"So why didn't you? Where were you?"

I froze. I couldn't speak. "I had an errand to run."

"What kind of errand? Where?"

"I was downtown with a friend." I tried to look him in the eye. "I'm sorry, am I under suspicion here?"

Fremont put the pad back in his pocket. "Excuse me," he said, nodding to a uniformed cop, who motioned me toward the open patrol car, offering me a seat in the back. I started to wave him off—then I saw a car pull to the curb, Simon Lefcourt's black Cadillac. Simon hadn't seen me yet—I turned my back as he hurried up the walk, gray-faced in the TV glare, turning around again to see the other cop from the hospital, Burke, easing him into the condo. Then there was Fremont again, hand on my arm.

"If you don't object, Mr. Hake, I have to go back to the station house."

Inside the condo, Burke was showing Simon Lefcourt his daughter's body. I fought back nausea. "I'm sorry, what?" I said.

"If you wouldn't mind following us down."

"To the station house."

"On Third Avenue. You know where that is?"

"Yes," I said, though I didn't. I didn't want to be there when Simon came out, I didn't want to see him at all.

"Mr. Hake?" said Fremont.

Hang in there, I thought. They're letting you back in your car, that means they don't intend to book you.

"And if you wouldn't mind riding with Officer Kaye."

"No, sir. That'd be fine." I didn't understand—I started toward my car, but Officer Kaye, half my age and twice my size, motioned me into a patrol car. My head was flashing—I saw Fremont talking to the TV people, I saw Simon slumped in a chair, staring at the wall. The trees riffled past. I tried to seal my mind over, muster every ounce of concentration. No use: first I kept seeing Simon's face, then blood on the carpet, then the bloodstain on Gwen's T-shirt. I tried thinking back to my first ride to a station house, back in Spokane, the lineup where Sandra Loyacano picked me out, all the stupid things I must have blurted out back then, none of which I could remember at this moment.

"This way, sir."

The station house was newly built, brightly lit, a few arrestees sitting on benches, hookers and drunks. The cop named Kaye put me in a room with a copying machine, leaving the door open. For a minute I felt lightheaded, about to lift off like a helicopter—I couldn't stay in my chair. Then I saw Fremont come in the main door, and I forced myself to stop pacing. He tapped on the doorjamb and came in.

"I want to thank you for coming down," he said, and quickly pulled up a chair.

"Did I have a choice?"

"Yes, you had a choice. Why, did you think you were under arrest?"

"No," I said. I looked at my wrist—there was the phone number Carl had given me. I wet my thumb and when Fremont was looking the other way I smeared it.

"I'm gonna order a sandwich, you want something to eat?"

"I'm fine," I said. Burke was coming in, with his red notebook. We nodded to each other. Fremont went back out into the open area.

"Exactly how long did you know the deceased?" said Burke.

What month is it, I thought. "I started working for her father—in April."

"When were you paroled again?"

"End of March."

"Okay. How did you meet her?"

Don't get down on yourself, I thought. They're testing you for consistency. "I told you how."

"Remind me."

"I did some work at her store."

"How long before the robbery?"

"Couple few weeks. We talked about this," I said to Fremont, as he came back in.

"Did we?" said Burke. "It's not in my notes. And your relationship with the deceased, how would you characterize it?"

I looked Fremont in the eye. "Nonexclusive."

"But you were intimate," he said.

I felt my breath start to leave me. Stay here, I thought. Don't let them bait you. "Yes," I said.

"You were aware of her reputation?"

"No," I said carefully. "What reputation?"

I watched a smile grow on Burke's face. "Fuck anything with a pulse," said Fremont.

"No," I said. I felt like strangling them both.

"You didn't know that."

"It's not true," I said. I was holding on tight.

"You have a key to her condo?" said Burke.

"No," I said.

Burke scribbled something in his notebook, showed it to Fremont, who nodded. "This friend you were having drinks with," said Fremont, "can you give us a ballpark on the time?"

I shrugged. "Before midnight."

"What about his name?"

Now it's time to shut up, I thought. "Mona."

"Mona what?"

"We never got to last names."

"Get her address? Her phone number?"

"No," I said.

"You sure her name wasn't Carl?"

I didn't budge. I stayed focused. "He's got nothing to do with this," I said.

"What's the last time you saw Carl Williams?"

I shook my head.

"I didn't hear that," he said.

"I don't know where he is," I said.

"He hasn't called your house?"

"Yes," I said. "You know he called my house, you've got it on tape. Are you gonna stop playing with me, or should I get myself a lawyer?"

"Good. Fine, you're right, let's cut out the bullshit. He sent you to a phone booth, and then what? First, why did you pretend not to know him? Was that for our benefit?"

"For my brother's," I said.

"Okay. So where did you meet up, you and Carl?"

"We didn't," I said firmly.

"Where is Carl Williams now?"

"I'm not going to say. I don't know."

"No. You were with this Mona. Come on, Denton, this could help you. What time did you get home?"

"Didn't look at my watch."

"Your neighbor says around midnight."

"My neighbor."

"April Hartigan."

I felt my chest tighten. "She's not the neighbor," I heard myself say. "She lives up the street. She walks the dog, she takes midnight strolls, she's retarded."

"What are you getting so testy about? Why are you picking up girls if you were engaged to the deceased?"

I blinked. What the hell was he talking about?

"Engaged?" I said. "*I* wasn't engaged to Gwen Lefcourt. Richard Nesbit's her fiancé. Was. They broke it off today."

I saw him wet his lips—he thumbed through his notebook, checking his notes.

"You need a moment?" I said.

He gave me a look. I tried to look over his shoulder, see what Burke was scribbling. I couldn't feel my heart beating at all, and then I realized where I was, across the room. Get back, I thought.

"I think I'd like to make a phone call," I said.

"Good," said Burke, clapping the notebook shut. "Good idea. I oughta warn you, Denton, we have an exact time of death, plus or minus fifteen minutes—where did you and 'Mona' have drinks?"

"A bar. I don't remember the name."

"You don't remember much, do you? Denton, I'm sure you know your rights, but I'm gonna tell them to you anyway."

I watched myself rise from the chair. You didn't do this and you know it. But I couldn't stop my mouth from moving. "I don't own a gun," I heard myself say. "I never have. I don't know how to use a gun."

At first I didn't realize what I'd said. Then I saw Burke flash Fremont a happy look, and my heart turned to jelly. When I spoke again, I could hear the terror in my voice.

"That's it. I'm not saying anymore."

"Come on, Denton. This was just getting interesting."

"Richard Nesbit owns a gun. That's why I said that."

"Okay."

"You oughta be talking to Richard Nesbit."

"Oh, we plan to," said Fremont. "Right now we're talking to you."

"No," I said firmly, digging in my pocket. I had

no change, and I'd given Carl every last bill in my wallet—when I looked up, there was Fremont handing me a quarter, signaling for a patrolman to show me to the pay phone. Outside I could feel it getting daylight. I dialed Elliot—Mimi answered after two rings. I could feel the phone in my hand, I was back and trying to stay back, and my heart was going a mile a minute.

"Elliot's not here," said Mimi. "Where are you? He's been frantic."

I could hardly speak. "I need to talk to him. Is he in his car?"

"The police were here again. They talked to April Hartigan."

Why this life, why me, I thought. "Page Elliot," I said. "I'm at the station house on Third Avenue, I'm in trouble. Okay? I'm sorry, Mimi."

"What happened?"

"Gwen Lefcourt was murdered."

Dead silence on the other end, but I could picture Mimi's nervous smile, like somehow this was good news. No, I was wrong—I heard her moan.

"Mimi?" I said. "I need to see Elliot." *I didn't do it.* Did I say it or just think it? "I didn't do it," I said quickly. "Could you page him, please?"

"Do you want to hold on?" she said. "I have to go up to your room to call him."

"Yes, I'll hold."

I was nowhere. I was spinning. Two minutes went by, then Mimi came back on the line.

"He's on his way over."

"Thank you, Mimi. Would you please do me one more favor?"

"Yes, anything. Of course."

"Call Dr. Nelson. Tell her I need to speak to her.

And please don't tell my mom yet." I hung up—the guard pointed me down the hall toward the fingerprint desk. You're fucked, was the look on my face. No, you're not. I wasn't that angry, I wasn't that jealous, I didn't hate her. The lockup door slammed shut. It was me and a kid in a tank top, half-drunk, and a homeless-looking guy asleep. I couldn't sit down, I was still too wired. There were bars around me again, and a shit smell everywhere—suddenly I felt like crying, crying and screaming, and I felt my body grow heavy and something heavy rising in my chest, grief and fear. I hugged myself hard, as though I could trap my spirit that way.

I wasn't going anywhere. I dozed off and nothing happened. When I looked up there was Elliot outside the bars. He just shook his head—didn't want to speak at first. They led us both to an empty room.

"Has it been on TV yet? Did Mom see it yet?"

"What did you tell these guys?" he said. He sounded angry.

I couldn't look him in the face, couldn't bear to admit my stupidity. "I said I didn't own a gun."

He cleared his throat. "I'm sorry, I don't get it."

"Okay. This is what happened. I drove to Gwen Lefcourt's house. I knew something was wrong, I couldn't get her on the phone, she was scared of Richard Nesbit, don't you remember I told you that? When I got there, the place was surrounded by cops. I started to lose track of time, I panicked, the next thing I knew I was running back to my car."

"Why?" he asked.

"I don't know," I said weakly. "I wasn't in control. The cops must have thought I was trying to leave—"

"You *were* trying to leave."

"No," I said.

"Denton."

"I wasn't running away. They just thought I was. And then I mentioned the gun—just now, when they questioned me—"

"Why didn't you ask for a lawyer?"

"Because I didn't do it! I swear to God! I was never inside her place tonight! I should have been, but I wasn't!"

"Then how did you know she'd been shot?"

"I just told you, Nesbit was after her. . . ."

I heard my voice trail off. I took a deep breath.

"Because I saw her," I said.

"You were there and you don't remember."

"No!"

"Then where were you? Where did you go when you left the house?"

I looked him in the eye. "Carl Williams. That's who called me, Carl Williams."

"Carl Williams," he said. "Oh Jesus."

"Listen, about Mom," I said.

"She doesn't know," said Elliot. The guard outside the door was calling his name.

"She's gotta know soon," I said. "She's going to see it on the news. I want to be the one to talk to her."

Elliot shook his head sadly. "Carl Williams," he said again, then rose from the chair and followed the guard back down the corridor while they marched me back to the holding cell. I curled up in the corner. The drunk guy in the undershirt was staring at me, slack-jawed, breathing in heavily through his mouth— he turned over and went back to sleep. The cell smelled of fresh piss. It's your fault Gwen's dead, I thought, if you hadn't been with Carl she'd still be alive—suddenly I felt so heartsick I couldn't bear it, but I knew I had to. I couldn't go anywhere, not with the questions they were asking and the blunder I'd already made, so to keep myself here I focused on a beetle, watching it crawl across the concrete, picturing what was going through its head and where it thought it was going, until at last a guard unlatched the door and called my name. They took me back down the hall—Elliot had returned, and now there was a boy in there with him, pink shirt and double-breasted suit, eyes like a Tartar behind rimless glasses. They were talking in low voices, I didn't get it at first, and then I saw his briefcase.

"Jordy Gillespie," he said, putting out his hand.

"Denton Hake," I said warily. So this was my lawyer, this 25-year-old kid.

"I've worked with your brother before," he said.

"I see," I said. He was blushing like a schoolboy.

"Elliot," he said, "maybe Denton and I should talk alone."

Elliot looked doubtful about this, but he left without a word. Jordy Gillespie pointed to the chair, inviting me to sit down.

"According to the police, you know what happened."

I was trying to size him up. Then I thought, it doesn't matter how tolerant he is of my condition, my gift, my curse, whatever. No reason he should understand, better if he doesn't. "Educated guess," I said.

"You assumed Richard Nesbit had shot her."

"Yes," I said tightly. And could you have stopped him? Without a gun? Or maybe you did have a gun and you don't know about it. No, I thought, don't start. You could have saved her life, but you didn't kill her.

Yes, and how can you be sure?

Jordy snapped open his briefcase. "Your brother says you have an alibi."

"It's worthless. The guy can't testify, he's an escaped convict. How old are you, Jordy?" I said abruptly.

He hesitated. "I'm thirty-nine."

I nodded. "You look twenty-nine," I heard myself say. "You'll probably be thankful for that as you get older, but at this point it's giving me the willies. How do you know Elliot?"

"My firm," he said, "represents your brother's company."

"Then you know he's not rich. And I don't have a dime. And neither does our mom."

The pouch under one of Jordy's eyes ticked lightly. "Don't worry about that," he said.

"Have you ever defended a murder case?"

"Yes," he said.

"Would I have heard about this case?"

"No. It was in St. Louis. I'm from St. Louis. I've defended three accused murderers."

"Successfully?"

"Yes. In two cases."

"Two out of three, is that respectable? I'm just asking."

"Mr. Hake, why don't we talk about your situation?"

"Denton," I said. I was thinking about Carl, what advice he would give me—you need to jolly this guy along, you've got to make sure he believes you. Some criminal lawyers, they get off on getting people off, the guiltier the better, but this guy wasn't of that breed. This Jordy Gillespie needed to know I was innocent. "The guy you want to look into is Richard Nesbit," I insisted. "He's violence-prone, and he's been getting weirder—buying guns, taking lessons. He called her a fucking whore, he screamed at her, in front of a hundred people, his own house. He was in a jealous rage. He told *me* he was going to kill her. He asked me to get him a nine millimeter pistol. What caliber gun did the killer use?"

He didn't answer right away—it was like he assumed I knew. "A .38. A rage over who?"

I'd already said too much about Carl, but I couldn't stop myself. "Carl Williams," I heard myself say. "Richard Nesbit thought she was fucking him."

"Was he?" said Jordy. His ears were reddening.

"I think Nesbit went there expecting to find them both. Maybe kill them both if he found them together."

"And that's why you told the police she'd been shot."

"Yes," I said. Any fool could see I was hiding something. He knows about your lapses, I thought, Elliot must have briefed him, he's blushing because he thinks you're nuts—and not just quirky nuts, downright crazy like how does this guy get through a day, the way I used to look at the headcases in prison, how did this one make his car payments, how does that one tie his shoes, if he can tie his shoes why can't he keep from molesting little boys? That's how Jordy Gillespie, boy lawyer, was looking at me. "Would you be willing to take a polygraph?" he said, too casually, still pink around the gills.

"Why, so you'll know whether to take the case?"

"Mr. Hake, I *have* taken the case." He closed his

briefcase. "You know, of course, your parole has been revoked."

"What a blow," I said. I sat there nodding while he explained how they'd try to set bail out of reach, and given Elliot's finances as he understood them, I'd probably be stuck in prison till the trial, how I wasn't supposed to talk to anyone from the District Attorney's office, what phone privileges I could expect, where in the county system I'd be confined, and so forth. They took me back to the cellblock, a private cell this time, six by ten. I tried to sleep, but no matter how I turned the wood cut into my bones. I couldn't let go, I couldn't relax—I was afraid of blurting something out, I had to be there for everything, the trip in the van to the county prison, the visit from the prosecutors. The guards doused me with bug spray, gave me a shower and a slightly larger cell where all the furniture was bolted to the floor. For dinner I got a Western sandwich through a slot, and a green salad with a cockroach in it, then a one-time-only trip to the PX, where I bought some toothpaste and some blank stationery and a pen, planning to write a note to Mom. Where was Richard Nesbit? I couldn't get near him, I was stuck inside my brain, thinking about Sandra Loyacano, thinking about my dad, reshuffling the old deck, Dad lying on the cellar floor, me and Elliot staring at him, Mom upstairs in the kitchen calling his name, Sandra Loyacano's thighs wrapped around my face.

I fell asleep with my head full of jail noises. Then at last I got loose, or so I thought—toward morning I felt myself rise from the cot and slip through the grillwork onto the corridor. The concrete was cold under my feet, and then I was back on my cot, dead awake. It was morning. I hadn't gone anywhere—

just a lucid dream, and a quick one at that.

Jordy and Elliot arrived after breakfast. They put us in a visitors' room, four long benches, nobody else in there.

"They know you were at her house," Jordy told me. "They have your fingerprints in her bedroom, in her bathroom."

"Old prints," I said. "From weeks ago. That's not a problem."

"They have a semen match."

"Ditto. Ask the girls at her store, they know we were doing it in the office."

"There's also evidence of rape."

I felt their eyes on me, cold and hopeful. My mouth opened but nothing came out.

"Genital abrasions," said Jordy. "They have the feeling it was postmortem."

My head started to swim. "Postmortem?"

"No flesh under her fingernails. No struggle. The blood was smeared on the carpet, indicating the body was moved after death. There's a couple of bloody shoeprints."

"They're not mine," I said.

"Well," said Jordy, "that's a negative we can't prove."

"Have they looked in Nesbit's closet? Have they checked out Nesbit's shoes?" The door opened—a guard came in, wheeling a polygraph machine on a cart. "That sick fuck, what does Nesbit say to all this?"

Jordy took a deep breath. "Nesbit's not here," he said.

"He's not here? You mean he's MIA?"

I saw Jordy and Elliot eye each other.

"He's in Minneapolis," said Jordy.

"Since when?" I said.

"Since eight p.m. that night."

"What night? The night she was killed? Bullshit," I said. "I don't believe it."

"Well, the prosecutors do," said Jordy.

Suddenly Elliot was in my face. "Denton," he said, "they're going to ask for first-degree murder."

I closed my eyes. Jordy was rattling away.

"—Frankly, that's not their druthers. It's political—once the media jump on this, the Loyacano rape charge is going to come out, which means from a perception point of view the state let a rapist out of prison and he went and shot a woman he was having sex with, so they can't ask for anything less than murder one, even though their case is entirely circumstantial, no eyewitnesses, and their physical evidence is too weak to show premeditation. What they do have is your virtual confession and your attempt to flee."

I opened my mouth, closed it, opened it again. "If Nesbit's got an alibi, it's bogus. And I can prove it."

I saw Jordy glance at Elliot. "How can you do that?" he said.

Just leave me alone, I thought. Just let me sleep.

"I can't bring up what you know about Nesbit," Jordy said, "without putting you on the stand. That leads to your past convictions, your episodes of amnesia, the whole dirty ball of wax."

I shook my head. "And I wasn't trying to flee," I said. I was starting to feel helpless again.

"You ready for the polygraph?" said Jordy.

"Where's Randy?" I said.

"She's waiting outside. She's going to administer the test, if that's all right with you."

"Why?" I said.

Elliot looked at me patiently. "Denny, it's just a dry run. Would you like us to leave?"

"Yes," I said. Jordy and Elliot went out and a few minutes later Randy came in, hair cut to the bone—it was like gray felt now, with spiky sideburns. For the first time she struck me as pretty. We were alone in the room except for the guard. Dark shapes were moving behind my eyes.

"I didn't do this thing," I said. "They think I did, but I didn't."

She didn't say anything to that. I watched her apply leads to my fingertips.

"I've been having thoughts about my dad," I said.

She looked at me sadly, like it might be too late for this now. "What kind of thoughts?" she said.

I tried to focus. "Hearing the shot from outside. And then going in the house with Elliot, and seeing my dad lying on the cellar floor."

She flipped on the polygraph machine. "And?"

"The gun is lying there, too."

"On the floor."

"You don't want to hear about this now, do you?"

"Of course I do. Can you stare at that spot on the wall?"

"You used to do this for a living, didn't you, give polygraphs," I said, watching Randy fiddle with the console. "You've been working for the cops all your life!"

She looked at me hard. "I'm trying to get a baseline."

"Yeah, right, okay, I'm sorry." I closed my eyes, tried to think green thoughts. I opened them again, staring where she wanted me to stare. "I like your hair that way."

"State your name, please."

"I'm having trouble leaving my body. Maybe because I'm remembering about my dad."

"Please state your name."

I gave my name, I gave Elliot's address, I gave my age. She entered some keystrokes.

"On the night of September fourth, did you visit Gwen Lefcourt at her condo?"

Visit, I thought. "No," I said. I tried to see the needle, whether it was going wild or not, but I was stuck inside my head.

"Where were you at eleven-thirty?"

"With Carl Williams."

"What kind of car do you drive?"

"Camaro."

"Did you kill Gwen Lefcourt?"

"No," I said.

"Where do you work?"

"Simon Lefcourt Construction."

"Were you in Gwen Lefcourt's condo that night or the next morning? Please try not to move."

"No," I said. It was hopeless—the needle had gone nuts, I could tell that from the look on her face as she headed for the door. Another ten minutes passed—if you'd held a gun to my head I couldn't have moved from where I was sitting. Then Randy came back, with Elliot and Jordy.

"I blew it, didn't I?" I said. They looked at each other, but before Jordy could speak I smacked the table. "It's bullshit, it's a bullshit test, it's the way the questions are worded. I *did* visit her, just not in the flesh. You don't believe me, fine. Just don't expect me to cop another plea."

"Denton, you're wrong," said Elliot, but of course that's just what was on all their minds. I heard my voice tense up.

"Dissociative defense. That's what you're thinking. You want me to say I was there, but my mind was someplace else. Guilty by reason of insanity, they lock me in a nuthouse, oh and then what, Randy comes to visit me, she hypnotizes me and I remember exactly how Dad died, every last gory detail, and that cures me, I don't forget things, that traveling stuff was all in my mind, I'm sane again and now they have to let me go. Which you and me and the state of Washington know will never happen in a million fucking years. No, frankly, I'll take my chances with the truth this time."

"But part of you thinks you're guilty—" said Randy.

"No!" I said. "Part of me was in her *condo*."

"—and the guilty part registered," Randy finished, pointing to the polygraph—not believing me for a second.

"Fuck you," I said. "Fuck all these tests. You think I'm Jekyll and Hyde, you think that machine proves it, well I'm not. I'll tell you what I might be," I said—hearing my voice fill the visitors' room. "I might be a whole new phase of human development, and that's why you've got to hang me."

They were dead silent, all of them.

"I think Denton and I should talk alone now," said Randy. Elliot didn't move, and Jordy was waiting for instructions. "Please," she said firmly.

Elliot and Jordy got up together and left the room. As soon as they were gone I saw Randy's look soften.

"I'm trying to see this your way," she said.

"Trying. Okay. That's something." At least she didn't say she believed me completely—I would've known she was blowing smoke.

''I brought you some medication.''

''What is it? Why?''

She took a vial out of her bag. ''It's Haldol.''

''No way,'' I said.

''Why not?''

''I knew guys in the joint who were taking Haldol. It's an antipsychotic.''

''It might make things easier.''

''Bullshit. It won't. My head's got to be clear, I've got to try and think back—isn't that what you told me? If I can't remember, they're going to hang me.'' I looked at the vial. ''Jesus,'' I said.

''What?''

''Nothing,'' I said. I was thinking about the pills in Mom's medicine chest, and the inhalers in Dad's night table, the cool breeze that filled your head when you snorted them. ''Just something Elliot told me.''

''What?''

''Drugs my parents used to take. Prescription drugs. My dad used to medicate my mom.''

''I understand,'' said Randy. ''But I'm not your dad.''

''Fine,'' I said. I was tired of arguing, and after she left I took one of the pills, but all it did was make my stomach churn. I kept seeing Dad moving on the cellar floor, his bleeding mouth, like he was trying to speak, the gun beside him—where was that coming from, why couldn't I remember more? I tried substituting something else, a flower, a mantra, just to shake my mind loose—I did push-ups, I focused on a spot on the wall, I tried hyperventilating, but nothing changed the picture in my head. I lay back on the bed, bracing for the sight of Dad's bloody face— suddenly my body lifted up, the moon raced through the branches, I was flying on my back through a grove of trees, twisting, turning, thrashing. Below was a bedroom, a girl's bedroom, an Axl Rose poster on the wall, and the girl from Richard Nesbit's party, naked except for her cutoffs, drawing coke lines on a vanity table. Nesbit sat down beside her, hair loose and in his eyes, and cupped her breasts, pinching her nipples hard between his thumbs and fingers. I rolled onto my face, drenched in cold sweat. A guard was knocking on my door.

"You have a phone call."

He unlocked the cell and plugged the phone into the wall.

"Denton?"

It was Mom. I tried to picture her. There were tears in her eyes.

"Mom, it's all right. Don't cry."

"I'm not crying."

"Yes, you are," I said. I could just make her out. "You're sitting there in a black dress and you're crying."

There was a silence. My head was still swimming with the sight of Richard Nesbit.

"I'm going to the funeral," she said. "I didn't know Gwen, but if you spent time in her company, she must have been a good person."

I let this go. "Yeah, she was," I said.

"You know," she said, "I was thinking back the other day. How you always knew people were coming to the house."

"Did I," I said. "I don't remember."

"You always knew when people were going to drop in."

I frowned. "When did this start?"

"What do you mean, when did it start?"

"After Dad died? Can I ask you something about Dad?"

She pretended like she didn't hear—Dad was the last thing she wanted to talk about. Forget it, I thought, tell her you need to call Elliot, Richard Nesbit's hiding out at his girlfriend's—but my brain wasn't listening. "Why did he do it? Why that day?"

"I don't know," she said. "Don't ask me."

"You were threatening to leave him, weren't you? And he got angry. He started threatening you. And then he went down to the cellar."

"You're asking this now?"

"Did Dot throw him over? Was he having financial problems? How depressed was he?"

"I don't want to talk about Dot."

"They had a falling out, didn't they. She went to work for another doctor, some of his patients left him, isn't that what happened?"

"Who told you this?"

"Elliot," I said.

"Denny, there's a lot of things you boys don't remember."

I was picturing Dad on the cellar floor. I saw his lips move. "Didn't he try and cry out to us? That's what I'm remembering."

"I think he knew he'd done a bad thing. Something he regretted."

"So he *did* call out."

"Denny, I'm going to pray for you," she said, in a small nervous voice. I thought, she wants to help but she can't, she believes you but she can't dwell on anything for more than two seconds, that's how she dealt with the pain all these years. I told her thanks and goodbye—the guard was about to unplug the phone in any case. I lay back, trying to keep my mind in the present, float back to wherever Richard Nesbit was hiding, but suddenly all I could think about was Gwen, the look of her, the smell of her, her confidence, her heedlessness, the waste. Then I was taking off my shirt. Why? At the moment I didn't have a clue, but that's the last thing I saw before I rose up, weightless suddenly, floating over treetops, a green lawn dotted with concrete. Cars were moving slowly up a driveway. I saw Simon Lefcourt's Cadillac, I saw Mom's Riviera pulling to the curb and Mom getting out, in a black dress and black shoes, and Bettina from Fay's Big & Tall, also in black. Richard Nesbit was nowhere in sight, but I could make out Simon Lefcourt. People were coming up to him, including a woman who looked enough like Gwen to be her mother. I saw her mouth moving, I heard her voice.

"—You did this."

Meaning, you brought this killer into her backyard. Simon Lefcourt didn't answer and the woman veered away, taking her place at the gravesite, far from her ex-husband and everybody else. For an instant I saw it all clear as day, and then the sky blinded me, the coffin sank into the ground—I saw myself roll onto my bed, naked to the waist, heard myself groan.

My shirt was in strips on the floor of the cell. I had one of the strips in my hands and I was knotting it around my neck, tying it so tight I couldn't breathe or scream or cry for help.

No!

My head smacked the wall behind the bed. I tore the cloth from my neck, choking and coughing, and flung it on the floor.

"Fuck," I said.

I sat up again, gulping for breath.

Crazy asshole! "You didn't do it. You didn't do it."

I whispered it over and over. My body thrashed on the bed.

"Dear God," I said. "Please don't let me give up."

I lay there talking to myself in the darkness—hoping to Christ I was listening.

12

The indictment came down—first-degree murder, bail denied. My plea date was set for the last week in September. Randy came as often as she could, Mom was still getting up her courage, Jordy and Elliot usually arrived together, especially if the news was bad. Jordy asked for a hearing to exclude my statement to the police, on the grounds I hadn't been properly Mirandized, but to no one's surprise the judge denied it.

"They're going to ask for the death penalty," Elliot told me.

"Of course they are," I said. "With the rape, it's an automatic."

"All it takes is one juror," said Jordy.

"Yeah, thanks," I said. I told them Nesbit hadn't come to Gwen's funeral. "Doesn't that strike you as weird, he was engaged to her and he stays away?"

It was like talking to the air. "If enough people believe you will walk," said Jordy, "you *will* walk."

"Jordy," I told him, "don't get mystical on me." I couldn't help teasing him, he got on my nerves, and I had no other outlet for my frustrations. Every night during jury selection I woke up gasping. They could hear me up and down the cellblock—I was starting to get a reputation. One day in the yard two black guys, both bald, one with tattoos of ankhs on his skull, sauntered over to me, handed me a green capsule and walked away. I didn't know if they were clowning around, if it was cyanide or cold medicine, but I flushed the capsule anyhow, just so I wouldn't be tempted while I wasn't watching out for myself. The plea date was approaching, no more visions of Richard Nesbit, and because of my night sweats and carrying on, I lost my phone privileges.

Then a week later I had a visitor. They took me down the hall, and there, rising to shake my hand, was Simon Lefcourt.

"I should have come sooner," he said, as we sat down.

"Sir, I appreciate it." I started to say something clumsy, but he stopped me.

"Denton, if I thought you were guilty I wouldn't be here."

"Yes, sir." His face was spongy with grief. "I know this took courage, I know your wife's down on you."

He looked at me sharply. "How do you know that?"

I was just making it worse. Then he said, "I suppose anyone would know that."

"Yes," I said.

"So what really happened?" he said. "Do you have any idea?"

"I have my suspicions," I said.

He had them, too. "Richard Nesbit?"

I nodded. "The night Gwen died, he was supposedly in Minneapolis. He's supposed to be there now, but he's shacked up with his girlfriend."

I was hoping he wouldn't ask me how I knew this,

and to my relief he didn't. Simon just sat there for a while.

"I asked Gwen to break off their engagement," he said at last.

He sounded so miserable I had to say something. "I think she was about to anyway," I said.

"They say his alibi is ironclad."

"Well," I said, "they're always ironclad until they're not."

"I plan to hire a private detective."

"Thank you. That's good to hear."

"It's for me as much as you."

"I understand." My time was up—before they led me away I asked him to check up on Jordy Gillespie for me. "He seems a little wet behind the ears."

He promised he would, but another week went by and I didn't hear from anybody. Mom was still avoiding me, and Elliot had to go to Portland on business. One night, as I was dropping off to sleep, gripping my pillow as if that would keep me from flying off, I saw him in bed with Mimi across his lap, massaging her shoulders, but the image was so wispy I couldn't tell if I was dreaming or if she really was back or if maybe she'd gone along on the business trip. When my phone privileges were reinstated, I called the house. Her outgoing message was still on the machine. I left a message for Elliot, urging him to coordinate with Simon Lefcourt on locating Richard Nesbit, then called Randy and asked her to come to the jail. She showed up a couple of days later—they let us meet alone in the visiting room. If she'd heard about my night terrors, she wasn't letting on. I eased into it by saying I'd been trying to spy on Richard Nesbit.

"And what's the problem?" she said—as if I'd just told her I was having trouble contacting Neptune.

"I'm scared to leave my body," I said, loud enough for the guard to hear—I didn't give a shit any longer who knew.

She guessed the reason. "Did you try to hurt yourself?"

"Yes," I said. "I'm afraid I won't get back in time. I only sleep in fits and starts, I'm scared to take drugs or masturbate, I even gave back my immersion heater. Funny, isn't it? You were right, part of my brain thinks I did it. My Dull Normal mind. And you all think I'm off the map, so where does that leave me? Have they asked you to testify?"

"It's been discussed," she said cautiously.

"But then they can put on *their* expert. I understand the dilemma. Then the memory lapses come into it. That's why I've got to locate Richard Nesbit. And I can't do that without putting myself at risk."

She listened patiently, then changed the subject. "Any more thoughts about your dad?"

I went along with her. "I remembered how the guy at the Exxon station used to call him 'Doc.' "

"And how did that make you feel?"

"Proud," I said.

"And the day he died? Have you thought any more about that?"

"Yes," I said. "I can't remember him dead."

"He's always moving."

"Yes," I said. She was about to try something, I could tell.

"Because he's still alive in you?" She said it quietly, like she didn't want to hurt my feelings.

"The suicidal guy, you mean?"

Whether she also meant, a guy who owned and used a gun, I didn't ask her, and talking about my dad didn't do anything for my confidence—the night she came to see me I slept with one eye open, so to speak, naked, no pillowcase, no sheets, with my clothes tied in a ball, all useless precautions but I couldn't just do nothing. Then the next day when I got back from the yard there was a guard outside my cell—Randy must have made a call to the authorities, because now I was on casual suicide watch. I closed my eyes, trying to concentrate on Richard Nesbit, but all I saw was misty twilight, the silhouette of a woman scraping the hull of a sailboat.

"Sometimes I feel maternal. Sometimes I'm just plain fascinated."

It was Randy's voice. The dock revolved below me.

"Worried."

"I'm trying not to be. He's got a weird kind of courage."

"Is he the strangest you ever treated?"

"Yes, and sometimes the sweetest. He knows about your taste in magazines."

"You're kidding."

"I wish."

"Are they going to make you testify?"

"God, I hope not. No."

That was that, just voices, Randy and her girl-friend, but hearing them suddenly, Randy's easy, playful tone, concerned but not too concerned, like my mom at her long-ago best, caused my own heart to lighten. I felt myself rise up, the entire city below me, all those lights coming on that spark God's envy, all those windows to peer into and the night sky roll-ing above me, the clouds and the moon, its bright dead face filling my eyes before I swooped down again, through the downtown canyons, wondering if Nesbit had an office here, flying past people making love in hotel rooms, dancing on rooftops, tooling out to sea in yachts. I was trying to get back to Randy, but now she wasn't at the marina with her friend, and Nesbit's parents' house was dark and his girlfriend's apartment was empty and the fog was rolling in—I heard myself whimper, I felt my head strike the wall of my cell. That's how it went, all the nights before my plea date, long flights through the city, sometimes calm, even exhilarating, but always ending in darkness and fog and a violent lurch that left me wide awake, unable to sleep for several hours, savoring what I could salvage of my travels and cursing their futility.

The date of my plea they hauled me over to the courthouse, gave me a suit to put on. Mom was in the courtroom for that—she had bought the suit—and Elliot too, but nobody else I recognized. Elliot came and sat at the defense table—I knew what was coming, or rather what they were hoping, that crazy as I was, I might have a sudden change of heart.

"How do you plead?"

The judge was in his fifties, jowly and hawk-eyed—his nameplate said William Driscoll. I started to speak, felt the lightness in my hands and feet, and sat down hard again without saying a word. How am I going to get through this, I thought. Then I bounced up again—the judge was about to say something to Jordy about my behavior, but this time the words came out of my mouth.

"Not guilty," I said. Elliot squeezed my wrist, gave me a smile—I started to think maybe I was wrong, maybe they believed me after all. After all, I was quite a handful—I had to bear that in mind.

Jordy rode back with me in the van.

"What happened in there today?"

"Nothing," I said. "I'm fine." Wait for the week-ends, I was telling myself. Give yourself time to get back, stay focused for court. "What's the judge's nickname?"

Jordy was staring out the back window of the van. "I'm not aware he has one."

"Hangin' Bill Driscoll? The Angel of Death? Irreversible Willie?"

He squinted at me through his yuppie glasses. "Are you going to be okay? Should I ask for a continuance?"

"On what grounds?" I said.

"Competency to stand trial."

He didn't really mean it, he was getting back at me for teasing him. "Jordy, I just pleaded not guilty, didn't you hear me?"

"Just barely," he said—wry as could be. They dropped us both off at the prison, and I didn't see him again until the first day of the trial. The sleepless nights began again, the afternoon naps with one eye open—I saw myself through the bars, but that was as far away from myself as I got. Think about Dad, I told myself, doctor's orders, try to remember the day of his death, start as far back as you can. I pictured Mom hunting for a suitcase, Dad yelling at her with the rose-clippers in his hand, saying he would do something drastic if she left, no way was he going to pay alimony, this was all Mom's fault, her paranoid imaginings, and meanwhile the phone kept ringing and Elliot kept answering. It was his nurse Dot on the other end, she mistook Elliot's voice for Dad's, I remembered Elliot telling me that—it was the first time Dot had called in months, she was trying to get back in Dad's good graces. But these were Elliot's recollections, all the details I was too young to process and too frightened to recall, no matter how many times I replayed them I couldn't make the memories my own, and by the time I came to court again I was bleary from no-sleep. Elliot was there, but no Mimi. Simon was there for the opening statements, so was Mom, plus some Lefcourt family members, all holding hands in the second row, but no woman who looked like Gwen's mother. Had I only dreamed the funeral? Was that all I could do now was dream?

"—condemned, out of his own mouth."

The prosecutor, Bell, was halfway through her opening statement. Where had I been? I looked around the courtroom, on the wild chance of seeing Richard Nesbit, but of course he wasn't there. I tried to stay put, size up the jury, keep my mind from wandering.

"—You will learn of the defendant's past criminal record—"

That much I caught, and I tugged at Elliot's sleeve. "How?" I said.

"Shh," said Elliot. He was watching Bell and now so was I, the way her skirt rode up in the back, exposing the veins behind her knees, and her hair, cut short and puckered like a shower cap, shrinking like a figure viewed from a balloon. She sat down, and I forced myself to focus on the jury, eight men, four women, all white, average age about 40—no peers of mine, I was thinking. And who exactly were my peers? Carl, my one friend. Gwen, God rest her soul. But these people, especially the women—it was like stopping at a traffic light and looking over at the next driver and thinking, she doesn't like the looks of you, you don't like the looks of her, you might as well be two different species. That's how the jurors struck me, the men as well as the ladies—suddenly I saw myself glaring at the jury box, and I made myself look away. It was Jordy's turn to talk—he was already on his feet, strolling in front of the jury, very slowly, first walking then talking, like he couldn't do both at once, and reciting from memory. I sucked myself back, forced myself to listen.

"—As I'm sure you could tell, the prosecution plans to lean heavily on my client's past record. This should tell you what they think of their own case. In a word—as I believe you'll soon discover for yourselves—it's weak. It's a feeble case. They don't have a weapon. They don't have a witness. They don't have a motive. What they have is a parolee. What they are counting on is your prejudice."

Memorized or not, it was a pretty good speech— who was I to be critical? I had all I could do to stay focused, keep one eye on myself, sitting there at the table, shoulders slumped, staring into space—from where the jury was sitting I looked like I was daydreaming.

And then I realized where I was.

Richard Nesbit's house was drifting below me.

I saw the oak trees, the gate, the pool, the picture window. Fool, I thought, you should have been staking this place out, there's no way you can kill yourself in court. Then I thought, well of course there is, all those eyes on me all the time, the judge, the jury, and again it was brought home to me, what hadn't escaped me at my first trial, that being in court is worse than jail, it's like school—look at the easels everywhere, the slide of Gwen lying in her own blood, and me slumped in my seat like I didn't care, with the jury checking me out to see how I was reacting, and I wasn't, I was trying to fight my way back into my head, thinking maybe they're right, maybe I don't give a shit, maybe I never did and I'm capable of anything and that's why she's lying there dead. At that point I heard myself gasp, a whimper came out of my mouth, and if anybody else was listening—that is, anybody except me, anybody on the jury—they must have thought, finally, finally some emotion, whereas in truth what I was feeling was despair, disgust at my willingness to give in like my dad to whatever shit was chasing him, guilt over cheating on my mom, money troubles, inability to be a proper father, or maybe just a black depression I would never be able to feel in my bones, because I always managed to be somewhere else when it descended. I shuddered, I hid my face—Jordy was giving me peculiar looks. There was Felix Ortega, big as life, on the witness stand—Bell, the prosecutor, was on her feet.

"Where are we?" I said.

Jordy leaned toward me. "Redirect," he whispered. I tried desperately to focus.

"—And where had he gotten this job lead?"

"In prison," Felix Ortega said. I looked sharply at Jordy, but he was underlining something in his notes—slowly, a wavy line, just doodling.

"Did you advise him not to see a Sandra Loyacano?"

I nudged Jordy's arm.

"Yes, I did," said Ortega.

"Why?"

Finally! Jordy stood up. "Objection. Outside the scope."

"Sustained."

Jordy sat down again. Bell was onto the Fay's Big & Tall burglary. Jordy let three questions go without objecting, and when I leaned over to whisper in his ear he leaned away.

"When you heard that a robbery had been committed," Bell was saying, "did you contact your client?"

"Yes," said Ortega.

"Why?"

"I wanted to make sure he hadn't done it."

I seized Jordy's wrist. "Objection. Calls for speculation," he said, like it hadn't occurred to him. Was I going to have to work his strings for the entire trial? Then how could I stake out Richard Nesbit? Whenever I let myself drift to Nesbit's, things in the courtroom jumped ahead without warning, so that either the lawyers were at the bench, or everybody was just sitting there waiting for God knows what to happen, or a witness was on the stand without having been sworn in, as far as I could recall. For example, now Bell was questioning Bettina, the Eskimo salesgirl.

"—And on that occasion, what did she tell you about the defendant?"

"She said she was afraid of him."

"She was terrified of him, wasn't she."

"Objection. Leading."

"Overruled."

"No, she never said she was terrified."

"Your witness," said Bell.

Jordy was shuffling his papers. At last he rose.

"Now when Gwen said she was afraid, what was her tone? Was she actually afraid, or was she bragging?"

My eyes filled with the color green. I saw Richard Nesbit's lawn, his gold Lexus pulling into the driveway. I sat there holding my head, like my soul was going to leak out through my ears.

"The People call April Hartigan."

I saw myself sit up, saw my mom lean forward, trying to catch my attention, smiling, shaking her head, as if to say, look who they have to call.

"Do you know the defendant?"

Stay focused, I thought.

"Everybody knows the defendant. He's the rapist."

The sudden hush rooted me to my chair. I'd heard enough to know what was happening—the prosecution had put April Hartigan on to blurt this out, and Jordy couldn't go after a retarded girl without appearing totally heartless. He was in a bind, that much I understood, but what I didn't understand was why Jordy was smiling, why he was nodding to himself—I saw him swap a look with Elliot, and he was nodding, too.

"Ms. Hartigan, on the night of the fourth, did you have occasion to speak to the defendant?"

"Yes."

"And what did he say to you? And what did you say to him? Just tell us in your own words, April."

Her mouth was moving. Richard's home, he's not going anyplace, stay here.

"—So at approximately midnight, thirty minutes after the time of death, give or take fifteen minutes, Denton Hake was just arriving home."

"Yes."

"No further questions."

"Mr. Gillespie?"

Jordy stood up. He had his gentle face on.

"April, do you know what today is?"

"Wednesday."

"And yesterday?"

"Yesterday what?"

"What did you do yesterday?"

"I walked the Fabricants' dog."

"When did you do that?"

I saw April's eyes widen into saucers. "From ten-thirteen to ten-forty-six. Then I walked the Millers' Collie at eleven-oh-two. Then at eleven-thirty I took a walk to the grocery store—"

She was chewing Jordy up and spitting him out. He stood there red-faced—whether she was some kind of idiot savant, or kept track of her comings and goings in a notebook, nobody had bothered to check. I couldn't take it anymore, what was the use, so what if I started screaming at my lawyer, he deserved it, I didn't belong here, I belonged at Richard Nesbit's. But there I sat. I couldn't get loose. I must have been squirming in my seat, because two or three jurors were checking me out, and then my head dipped forward and his lawn tilted below me like a pool table.

I heard the sound of a shovel clanking against a rock.

Then there was Nesbit, plain as could be.

He was digging a hole.

The dirt sprayed up against the sky, the sun fell below the roof, a half-moon appeared above the oak trees. I floated with him toward the house, through the darkness and into the courtroom.

There was nothing. I wasn't there. The courtroom was empty. For a moment I was totally panicked, not knowing how much time had elapsed, hours or days, it was like coming home and finding your apartment house burned to the ground—then I saw the windows were black, the half-moon was still there in the sky. I saw myself lurch up from my cot, run to the bars of my cell.

"I need to talk to my lawyer." I was practically shouting.

The guard came and went away.

I sat down on my cot, holding my head, trying to

get loose again. I saw the green haze of Nesbit's lawn, but that was all. When I looked up, Elliot was sitting across from me in the visitors' room.

"Denton," he said.

I was back. I stared at him.

"I saw Richard Nesbit," I said. "He was at his parents' house—the house where he threatened Gwen, where he beat her up."

He looked back at me evenly. "What was he doing?"

"He was digging a hole. There's a planter in the yard behind the swimming pool. Get somebody out there—call Simon Lefcourt."

"What do you expect us to find?"

Suddenly I felt like Dad—I wanted to take the flesh of Elliot's wrist and twist it till he screamed. "Elliot, he was burying the gun! And his bloody shoes!"

"You saw that," he said.

I didn't want to lie. "I saw him digging."

"You remember he has an alibi."

"Yes, I remember. Minneapolis."

"The Airport Sheraton," he said.

"Says who, the computer? He was checked in there, doesn't mean he *was* there."

"They have a Minneapolis ATM receipt. When Gwen Lefcourt was shot, he was withdrawing money from his checking account."

"At the very moment she was shot?"

Elliot sat back frowning. "I see what you're getting at."

"You see now? Pretty convenient."

"He could have mailed the ATM card to somebody."

"There you go," I said. "Or his girlfriend could have gone to Minneapolis."

"And taken the card with her." Elliot was nodding.

"Elliot," I said, "if I could pick up a shovel, I'd be there. But that's why I need you."

"What you need is a warrant," he said doubtfully. "What's our probable cause, you saw it in a dream?"

"It wasn't a dream," I said. "I wasn't asleep, I was in court."

"Whatever. Denny, we've gotta do better than that. What's Nesbit doing now?"

I closed my eyes. What I saw was Dad's body on the cellar floor, me and Elliot standing over him. Blood was dripping from Dad's mouth and he was trying to speak. Where was the bullet, was it really in his face? And where was the gun, why was it so far away? "I don't know," I said weakly. "I can't always focus."

Elliot rubbed his palms on his knees. "I'm going to call Simon Lefcourt," he declared. He was halfway between believing and not believing, and pitying me all the same, for which I could hardly blame him. He didn't return that weekend, sending a message through Jordy that he had contacted Lefcourt and was engaging his private detective. Monday morning he was back in the courtroom, the day Fremont played for the jury my message on Gwen's machine. Randy was there, too—I wondered why for a moment, then made myself focus.

"—So the defendant could have put a bullet through Gwen Lefcourt's heart, and later called to see how she was, in a misguided attempt to supply an alibi—"

"Objection, calls for a conclusion," said Jordy. This time I didn't have to prompt him.

"Sustained."

"Could he have forgotten he committed the murder, and that's why he placed the call?"

"Objection. Ms. Bell is grandstanding."

"Sustained."

The next recess they took me to a holding area—Jordy and Elliot were there, along with Randy. Something was up—a kind of hopeful hush greeted me as I entered.

"This came for you," said Jordy. It was an envelope, no return address, sliced open by the prison. Inside was a card, a cartoon of a building labeled CRISIS CLINIC going over a waterfall, in flames. HANG IN THERE, said the caption.

"Do you recognize the handwriting?" asked Jordy.

"No," I said. Did they think it was from Carl Williams? Then I looked at the postmark.

It said Spokane.

"It's from Sandra Loyacano," I said. "This is great. This is proof," I said to Randy, to all of them.

"Proof of what?" said Jordy.

"Are you kidding? The girl I was accused of raping, and here she's sending me a get-well card. She heard the rape charge came out in court, and she feels guilty, she knows she only hollered rape because she invited a thief to have sex with her. You see?" I said to Randy, waving the envelope. "I wasn't making it up, I'm getting my memory back. You have to call her—"

"Denton, we tried calling."

"And?"

Elliot shook his head. "She doesn't live there anymore."

"Then who sent this card?"

"We don't know," he said. "We thought maybe you could tell us."

Did they mean Carl? But Carl was in Canada. My heart sank again. They were hopeful about something else—for the life of me I couldn't make out what. "What did you find at Nesbit's place?" I asked.

Elliot didn't say anything. I got the feeling the others were waiting for him to speak.

"Simon Lefcourt's P.I. went out there," said Elliot.

"And?"

"And nothing."

"Did he dig up the planter?"

"Denny, we're talking about the Fourth Amendment here—"

"Fuck the Fourth Amendment! Did they check to see if he had planted something? He could have put something in the hole, a shrub, a bush. Iron is good for plants, remember, Elliot? Dad used to make us put nails in the ground, to keep all the leaves green? Sure, you remember. The only green leaves in Richard Nesbit's garden, that's where the gun is."

I finally stopped myself. A kind of relief rippled through them all: he's around the bend, we don't have to listen to his bullshit anymore. Randy and Jordy were silent, waiting for Elliot to tell me what they had to tell me.

"Denny, they're ready to cut a deal."

Where did this come from, I thought. And then: Oh God, it's worse than I imagined.

"Who is?" I said carefully. Suddenly I was very scared. "What deal?"

"You'll be allowed to change your plea. Not guilty by reason of insanity."

"I see," I said.

"You see?"

"Right," I said—cool as could be. "How about nolo contendere by reason of insanity?"

They looked at me blankly.

"I don't know if I did it," I explained, "therefore I'm not putting up an argument."

Randy was looking in her lap. She might think I was certifiable, but at least she knew when I was being sarcastic.

"Yes," said Jordy, "but we've already put up an argument."

"Yeah, so it's like, I don't remember doing it, because the deed is abhorrent to me, therefore don't believe a word of it, this guy is trying to squirm out of the noose, don't send him to the nuthouse they'll only cure him, just string up his ass and be done with it. Adios, Denton."

"You don't understand," said Elliot.

"And I thought you were starting to believe me," I said, looking at Randy. "I guess I was wrong."

"It doesn't matter what we believe," said Elliot. "The point is, they're willing to take it away from the jury."

"Isn't that nice," I said. "And you actually heard them out on this."

"And send you to a facility."

"A facility. How thoughtful. Randy, I assume they've cleared this with you? Sure they have, you always thought I was guilty. Not to mention psychotic."

Her face tightened. "I never said you were psychotic."

"Your girlfriend thinks so. I didn't get a good look, is she pretty?"

I saw her temple vein throb.

"Denny, try and focus," said Elliot. "The minute you're cured you're a free man. And—" he said, eyes widening, the good part was coming, "—they're willing to take Randy's word for *when* you're cured."

I frowned. "In return for what?" I asked.

Jordy and Elliot shared a look, each waiting for the other to speak.

"Carl Williams," said Jordy.

I looked at them blankly. As crazy as I might be, I wasn't crazier than the rules that put me here.

"They're convinced Carl Williams did the Fay's Big & Tall robbery," said Elliot. "They allowed this guy to escape, and they're getting all kinds of flak. If you can deliver Carl Williams, they're more than willing to show their gratitude."

Gratitude? "Elliot, even if I could 'deliver' Carl Williams . . ."

Elliot suddenly gnashed his teeth. "Oh for Christ's sake," he sputtered. "Here we are, trying everything we know how to get you off—"

"I didn't do it, Elliot. And I am getting off."

"Oh, what did you do now, travel to the future?"

"Guys, could we all try and lower our voices," said Jordy.

"What do you owe this jungle bunny? Did you get married in prison or what? Denny, this guy's a career criminal, he sticks guns to people's heads. What's his fucking excuse, why are you defending him—Denny?"

"What?" I said. Suddenly Elliot was leaning across the table at me, eyes boring in.

"How do you know Carl Williams didn't kill her?"

The room fell silent.

"I said," Elliot insisted, "how do you know Carl Williams didn't kill Gwen Lefcourt?"

I didn't know what to say. Then it dawned on me, what all this was about. I looked carefully at Elliot.

"You're running out of money, aren't you?"

He clicked his teeth. "This is the last chance they're gonna give us, Denny. If we say no, they go for the nuts."

"How broke are you?"

He shrugged. "Broke enough."

"Did you tell that to Simon Lefcourt? Did you ask him to help out?"

The grayness under Elliot's eyes seemed to darken. "Denny, he's starting to have his doubts, too."

"Too?" I said. "Too?"

I don't know why it surprised me—maybe because nobody had actually said they thought I'd done the murder.

"Okay," I said. "I get it."

They looked at me, Elliot and Jordy, waiting for me to go on. Randy had turned away, like she knew what I was going to say next. If so, she knew more than I did—it wasn't until I heard it come out of my mouth that I realized what I was saying.

"I want to testify."

I was staring across the table at my face. Jordy started to say something, but Elliot held up his hand.

"No," he said. "No way."

It was out, I couldn't take it back, and maybe I was right. "It's my call," I said. They were across from me again.

"Denny, it's suicide," said Elliot.

"Why? You afraid I'm going to confess?"

Nobody said anything.

"I didn't do it, Elliot. Richard Nesbit did. And I can smoke him out."

They all looked at each other. Of course they'd discussed this among themselves, but Elliot was frowning like he was hearing it for the first time.

"You realize how big a can of worms this is?" he said.

"Big," I said.

"They're going to ask you your alibi on cross," said Jordy.

"What if you space out?" said Randy.

"Don't worry about me," I said. "I'll *be* there and I'll *stay* there." That was one part hope, nine parts hollow bravado—for her part, Randy was nodding encouragement, and I was grateful for that. "Just make sure to ask me about Richard Nesbit," I said to Jordy.

"Well, of course," said Jordy. "And you have to answer about Carl."

"I'm going to say, I was having drinks with a friend, I don't know how to reach him. I'll name the hotel because he's not gonna be there. And that's all I'm gonna say, because that's all I know."

Elliot and Jordy shared another look. They didn't believe that for a moment, but they weren't going to push it.

"All right," said Elliot. End of discussion—we all stood up. Elliot started toward the door, then turned back and gave me a bear hug, holding me tight until Randy and Jordy were out of the room. Then, without another word, he followed them out.

I went back to my cell.

I lay down, closed my eyes, trying to calm myself. "Carl?"

He was sitting across from me. Randy was taking

notes, Carl was passing a bottle around, the deck of her girlfriend's sailboat was teeming with tiny creatures—a dream, pure and simple. The shower bell was ringing. I shuffled out onto the run. The two bald black guys, the ones who had given me the capsule, eased up on either side of me.

"We just want you to know. Carl has faith."

We, I thought. I didn't say anything, I looked away.

"He knows you're a good man, just to relax." He patted my ass, bared his teeth, and they walked away again. I returned to my cell. There was extra food waiting, roast beef and gravy. I couldn't eat. I lay down and drifted out through the mesh, savoring the night air, the illusory freedom. There it was below me, the house, the patio, Elliot and Mimi holding hands, smooching in the open air. No more doghouse, that was for sure—but when they came up for air he looked troubled, gray pouches under his eyes, mouth hanging open. I watched Mimi head into the main house, unzipping her sundress. Elliot turned and walked up to the garage. I saw him climb the stairs, then lie facedown on my bed, head sandwiched between two pillows. In the moonlight, the shadow of the garage lay across the driveway, all the way to Elliot's Camry.

A shot rang out. I sat up with a gasp.

I didn't know where I was, where I'd just been, or whether I'd just been dreaming, or if I was still in the dream. I saw Dad's gun on the cellar floor and a hand picking it up and then the gun barrel going into his mouth. The gun went off again. Dad's head fell back onto the concrete. This time he wasn't moving.

13

Do you swear to tell the truth, the whole truth, and nothing but the truth, so help you God.''

"I do," I said.

"Please state your name."

As soon as I said it I felt my head loosen. To keep myself focused I slid forward in the chair until I was in danger of falling on my ass, concentrating on Jordy's face—he was running through the standard questions, my address, occupation, and so forth, with a grim fixed expression designed to keep me on point.

"Did you hear the testimony of April Hartigan?"

Was that his first question? I wasn't sure. It seemed to be coming from left field.

"Did you hear her refer to you as a rapist?"

"Yes," I said. Be careful, I thought.

"You never raped anybody, did you?"

"No."

"You didn't rape Gwen Lefcourt."

"No," I said.

"Did you kill Gwen Lefcourt, Mr. Hake?"

"No," I said. So far so good.

"Where were you the night she was murdered?"

I saw my hand reaching for the water glass. Big

mistake, and I tried to stop, too late. The glass never made it to my lips—I saw my arm tremble and jerk, and water spilled out onto the witness box. I saw Randy close her eyes and bow her head. I saw Simon Lefcourt in the back of the courtroom and Elliot in the front, both staring straight at me.

"The St. Regis Hotel."

"And what were you doing there?"

"I was visiting Carl Williams."

"And what was the purpose of your visit?"

I looked Jordy in the eye. "Just to see him again."

"Do you know where he is now?"

"No," I said firmly. I checked out Elliot, but his expression hadn't changed either. Randy was the only one shifting around, the only one who looked at all worried.

"And what time was this?"

"Between eleven, twelve o'clock."

"Are you aware that eleven-thirty p.m. is the approximate time of death?"

"Yes," I said.

"At eleven-thirty p.m., you were with Carl Williams?"

"Yes, sir."

"Then where did you go? Did you go to Gwen Lefcourt's house?"

I looked at Randy. "No. I went home."

"Where you ran into April Hartigan on the street."

"Yes, that's right."

"When you got home, what did you do?"

"I called Gwen Lefcourt," I said.

"Why?"

"I was worried about her," I said.

"Why were you worried, Mr. Hake?"

I looked at Randy—she was squirming in her seat, like she was about to leave the courtroom herself. "Because of Richard Nesbit."

"I'm sorry, I don't believe we heard that."

"Richard Nesbit," I said, "had made threats against Gwen's life."

"Objection," said Bell. "No foundation."

"Sustained."

"Do you know a man named Richard Nesbit?"

"Yes. Her fiancé."

"Was Richard Nesbit jealous of your relationship with Gwen Lefcourt?"

"Objection as to relevance."

"Sustained," said the judge. He was motioning Jordy and Bell toward the bench. I looked out at Randy, trying to smile, trying to keep myself anchored. I could feel myself slipping away, and the worst was yet to come. Jordy walked back to the defense table.

"No further questions," he said.

What?

I stared at Randy—she leaned forward in her seat to ask Elliot a question, but he waved her off, shaking his head.

What had I missed? Why were they giving up so soon?

"Ms. Bell?" said the judge.

I was halfway out of my chair, struggling to sit down again—the judge was saying something, a murmur was going through the courtroom. Then I was back in my seat, with Bell's face in front of mine, pale mouth and piercing eyes.

"Where did you meet Carl Williams, Mr. Hake?"

I waited for the objection. Jordy just sat there. Randy was still trying to get Elliot's attention, but

Elliot had moved into the chair next to Jordy.

"Did you understand the question, Mr. Hake?"

"In prison," I said.

"And what were you serving time for?"

"Burglary and assault."

"Mr. Hake, do you recall discussing with Gwen Lefcourt the state of her finances?"

In the back of the courtroom, I saw Simon Lefcourt lean forward. His eyes were closed, he was rubbing his forehead. "Yes," I said.

"Did she tell you her insurance was about to lapse?"

I looked at Elliot sitting next to Jordy. His jaw was set and he wasn't blinking. "Yes."

"And you're aware her store was broken into on the night of July seventeenth."

"Yes," I said.

"Mr. Hake, did you break into her store?"

I clenched and unclenched my fists. "No," I said.

"Let me put it another way. Do you remember breaking into her store?"

"Objection. Mr. Hake has just answered the question."

"Sustained."

"Why did you go to see Carl Williams that night?"

"Because he asked me to."

"Did he ask you for money?"

I felt myself begin to weaken. "He may have."

"On the night of September fourth, do you remember withdrawing four hundred dollars from your savings account?"

I glanced at Elliot again. I started to say I didn't recall, then I stopped myself. "Yes," I said.

"And do you recall giving it to Carl Williams?"

I looked in my lap. "Possibly," I said.

"Yes or no, did you give the money to Carl Williams."

"I don't remember."

"You don't remember. And where is Carl Williams now?"

I looked up into Bell's eyes. Behind her I could see Jordy and Elliot, just sitting there, trying to look nonchalant and not succeeding. And where was I? I was watching my lips, waiting for the word Vancouver to come out of my mouth, as if I had no choice in the matter—damn you, I thought, get hold of yourself, and I was looking out through my eyes again.

"I don't know," I said. That's better, I thought, and looked over at Elliot. He sat there without blinking.

"Mr. Hake, is Carl Williams your lover?"

I heard some rustling from somewhere, the jury box, the defense table, and then my own voice speaking the truth. "Not that I recall," I said.

I saw Randy's eyes close. I saw my own eyes close. I was picturing Dad with his belt off, standing in his bedroom doorway.

"I'm sorry, Mr. Hake, I'm not sure the jury heard that."

I was back in. "No," I said.

"But Gwen Lefcourt was your lover."

"Yes," I said.

"Was she also Carl Williams's lover? Do you know? Do you recall that?"

"Yes," I said. "And also Richard Nesbit's."

"Just answer the questions I ask," said Bell. "Now, after you left the St. Regis Hotel, you say you went straight home."

"I went home, yes."

"Straight home? Or don't you remember?"

"I remember I went home."

"You didn't go to Gwen Lefcourt's house?"

The courtroom started to revolve. I was seeing Dad again. "I went later on."

"Well, but you said you were worried about her. If you were so worried about her safety, why wouldn't you keep your date with her?"

My mouth opened. Nothing came out. The room was spinning slowly. I was seeing Dad and Elliot, yelling at each other, Dot behind Dad in the bedroom doorway.

"Were you angry with her, Mr. Hake?"

"No," I said.

"No? Isn't it true you were insanely jealous of Carl Williams?"

"No," I said. "Richard Nesbit was jealous of Carl. He was jealous of us both."

"Are you aware, Mr. Hake, that Mr. Nesbit was in Minneapolis the night Gwen Lefcourt was murdered."

"His ATM card was, that doesn't mean *he* was—"

"—that the police have four samples of Mr. Nesbit's handwriting, all taken from credit card receipts in the Minneapolis area?"

I watched my eyes close. In my head I saw Dad moving toward Elliot, belt in his hand. I forced my eyes open again. "No, I didn't know that," I said.

"Mr. Hake, does the name Sandra Loyacano ring any bells?"

"Objection as to relevance."

"Sustained."

"You don't remember assaulting her?"

"Objection!"

"Mr. Hake, do you know what a polygraph is?"

"Yes," I said, looking hard at Elliot. Dad was snaking the belt around his neck.

"Have you ever taken a polygraph in connection with the events of this case? Do you recall?"

I waited for Jordy to object. He didn't move a muscle. "Yes," I said.

"But we haven't heard from your attorney concerning the results of that test."

"Objection," said Jordy. "Attorney-client privilege."

"Withdrawn. Mr. Hake, have you ever sustained any head trauma?"

"Yes," I said. Elliot was having trouble breathing. Dad was tightening the belt around his neck.

"As a child? Were you abused as a child?"

"I saw some things," I said. Elliot's eyes bugged out with fear.

"What do you mean, you saw some things?"

Dad was smiling, Dot was screaming.

"Mr. Hake?" said Bell.

"I saw my father die," I said, looking over at Elliot again. He stared back, jaw set, like he knew exactly what was happening in my head. In my mind's eye I saw him scramble down the hall into his room and slam the door.

"What about recently? Were you in an automobile accident recently? And did you lose consciousness for several days as a result?"

"Yes," I said.

"Do you ever suffer from blackouts?"

"Depends what you mean by blackouts."

"Do you have episodes in which you seem to leave your body?"

"Yes," I said. My eyes were locked with Elliot's.

I saw the gun on the cellar floor, and then the gun in Dad's hand. Dad was trying to speak, and then came the gunshot.

"And when did this start?".

"In the hospital."

"Before that, you simply had problems with your memory?"

"Yes," I said.

"And when you seem to leave your body, do you lose control over your body's activities?"

Mom was upstairs, behind the cellar door. I was next to Elliot. Dad was bleeding on the floor. His mouth was moving, he was pleading for my help. Don't let me die, he was saying. "I never killed anybody," I said.

"At your first trial, you didn't remember raping Sandra Loyacano—"

"Objection!"

"Sustained. Ms. Bell, the next time you stray into this area, I'm going to hold you in contempt."

"—and you don't remember robbing Gwen Lefcourt's store. You don't remember visiting Gwen Lefcourt's condo, you say you were never inside, and yet you knew—without setting foot inside her place or looking in her window—that she had died of a gunshot wound to the heart. You knew she had been murdered, even though you went straight from the St. Regis to your brother's house—"

"I knew Richard Nesbit owned a gun. It was a logical assumption—"

"—or perhaps your body went to her house and you don't remember. Is that possible, knowing what you do about yourself? Is that what you're asking us to believe?"

"No—"

"So what are you asking us to believe?"

The gun was on the floor. Dad's eyes were asking me to help, but I was somewhere else. Then the gun was in his mouth. "I saw her dead," I said.

"Without being there."

"Yes," I said. Tears sprang to my eyes. I turned to the jury, as if to show off my tears, but that wasn't my intention. I had something I wanted to say, and no force on Earth, including my own vigilance, was going to stop me. "That's just something I can do. I'm not proud of it. I never wished it on myself. We all have things we don't remember doing, but there are things we know we couldn't do in a million years, because no matter how confused we get, we know who we are. We know if we're capable of cruelty, or lying, or thievery. And I have been a thief, I don't deny it. I don't blame anyone for that except myself, I'm nobody's victim, and just because I was trying to help people at the time, or thought I was, that doesn't justify stealing, and I'm not asking for anyone's forgiveness but my own. I'm what you see, a scattered individual, but I'm not capable of rape and I never killed anyone. If there's murder in *your* heart, so be it," I said, circling myself as if I were an airport, unable to land, and picturing, suddenly, my head in a sack and a noose around my neck, hoping the jury might be persuaded to think of that as well, "but don't condemn me to death because you can't trust your own impulses. If you're capable of something I'm not, live with it, try and understand it, but for God's sake don't make *me* the bad guy."

I heard myself break off. Randy was looking at the floor. Simon Lefcourt was rising from his seat. I sank back into myself, staring at Elliot—I might have been looking toward his chair the whole time.

"No further questions," said Bell.

I shut my eyes. The gun was back in Dad's hand, and Elliot was curling his index finger around Dad's.

"Mr. Gillespie?"

I saw Jordy glance at Elliot, I saw Elliot shake his head no, then shade his eyes. Yes, at long last it was dawning.

"Your Honor, the defense rests."

Noise bloomed in the courtroom. I saw myself get up from the witness chair, walk over to the bailiff and out the courtroom door, without looking at Randy, Mom, or Elliot. The van door slammed, the prison gate opened. A guard was leading me back to my cell. I saw myself lie down on my cot. My shoulders were shaking, then my body was still, and then I was on my knees in front of the toilet, tears streaming down my face. The shower bell rang. The two black bald guys were shaking my hand. Everybody on the wing was proud of me. Everybody was singing my praises. In the mess hall I watched myself stare at my plate without eating, then followed myself back to my cell. I lay down on the bed. I waited until my breathing grew shallow and my eyeballs began to move behind my lids and then I left myself alone, lowering through the branches of the pine trees toward my brother's house. In the bedroom Elliot and Mimi were going around the dial. There was a bottle of wine on Elliot's night table. Evidently they'd already made love, because they were in T-shirts and underwear. The TV went off, and the bedroom lights. I watched Elliot lie there staring at the ceiling, then get up and put on his robe and slippers. In the kitchen Ozzie stirred, then went back to sleep. I watched Elliot go out the back door and up the driveway to the garage. He went slowly up the stairs into my room.

I watched him kneel down, pry up the floorboard.

Underneath was a .38 revolver.

My eyes snapped open.

The guard was knocking on my cell door. It was morning. Nausea was clawing at my throat.

They took me in the van to the courthouse. I looked around for Elliot, but he was late. There was nobody but Jordy and Bell. I tried listening to the summations, but they were the same as the opening arguments, just different language. Then the judge was speaking.

"I want to be very clear on two points," he was saying. "A verdict of guilty means you are prepared to put this man to death. Secondly, this defendant did not plead insanity, and whatever impressions you may have formed about his mental condition should have no bearing on your verdict. Did he commit this crime or not? That's what you're being asked to decide."

The jury filed out. I watched the bailiff put on my cuffs. I watched the guard escort me down a hallway to a visiting room. Mom was waiting in one of the chairs. I saw her take my hands and wring them. Then I was looking into her eyes.

"Didn't Elliot come with you?"

"He'll be here," she said. "He's coming. This has been hell for him, too."

I had to smile at that. "Hell for everybody," I said.

"Denton, you can't lose faith. You're God's child, he gave you power for a reason."

"I'm starting to feel like His delusion." I could see Elliot's Camry pulling up to the prison gate. My heart pumped fiercely. Steady, I thought.

"You know Elliot's out of money," she said.

"Yes," I said. "This trial didn't end a minute too soon, did it?"

Her eyes searched my face. "What do you mean?"

I was seeing the floorboard in my room. It was back in place again. "He never did try to contact Sandra Loyacano, did he?"

She stared back at me blankly.

"Can I ask you something, Mom? About the day Dad died?"

Mom shook her head. "I've always told you, Denton, I don't remember very much."

"Neither do I. But it's been coming back, you know? The fog, it's clearing. Do you remember the two shots? You remember when Dad called out to you?"

She shut her eyes. "I'd rather not talk about this," she said. "For me it's still a blur."

"Elliot filled in the details."

"As much as I could take."

"Yeah, exactly. Me, too. Everything I used to know about that day, I heard from Elliot. And speak of the Devil," I said clicking my teeth together—I was watching Elliot walk down the corridor. Outside the holding room he halted, putting on a long sad face before entering. The door opened—he pulled up a chair next to Mom.

"It's looking good," he said. "They say the jury's due back before nightfall."

"Why is that good?" I said. My hands started to shake.

Elliot sighed. "Ever the pessimist."

I looked him in the eye. "Mom, would you mind leaving me and Elliot alone?"

Mom shot a look at Elliot. He squeezed her arm,

nodding. She rose, leaned over to give me a kiss, and
went out the door—as Elliot put on a grim smile, I
felt myself drift after her, looking for the jury room.
I saw the jury changing seats—evidently somebody'd
been elected foreman, and was taking his place at the
head of a conference table, but I couldn't make out
what he looked like, merciful or impatient, because
Elliot was leaning toward me now.

"—I *liked* what you said in there," he was saying.
"I'm *glad* you spoke up for yourself."

"Couldn't help myself," I said.

He thought that one over. "It's been torture, hasn't
it."

"It's had its moments," I said.

He gave me his priggish look. I felt like wrapping
my hands around his throat. "Hasn't been easy for
me, either," he said.

"Yeah, that's what Mom said. But at least Mimi's
back to stay," I added, leaning toward him. Watch
yourself, I thought. "Couple of things I'm fuzzy on,"
I said.

"You?" said Elliot amiably. "Fuzzy?"

"How exactly did you find Jordy Gillespie?"

He sighed. "Don't you remember? He did some
work for the firm."

"Uh-huh," I said. "And what's in my room?"

"What's in your room? What do you mean?"

"Under the floorboard now."

He made a face. "I don't know what you mean.
Mimi's bottle of brandy?"

"Is that Dad's .38 under there?"

He cocked his head as if he hadn't heard me. I
was picturing the two of us side by side, bending over
Dad's dead body. "You know who I blame in all
this?" said Elliot.

"Who?"

"I blame your therapist."

"You do? For what?"

He didn't answer. He looked at his hands. "This leaving your body nonsense. She helped foster that delusion."

"Also, I didn't remember about Dad."

"Well, that's what I'm saying," he said. But he was watching my eyes now.

"I *was* deluded," I said. "About Dad's death. But I had you to thank for that."

His eyes stayed on my face. "All right," he said. "If you want to keep talking nonsense. I don't think you realize what's at stake here, do you? I don't think you've ever realized."

"I'm a pretty cold fish, aren't I?" I said.

"You *are* cold sometimes."

Dad's eyes were cold. Two shots, and now there was a bullet in his brain. "Like Dad."

"In some ways, yes." I saw him glance down at his watch.

"Dad was totally cold. Totally self-centered. Unlike you."

"Well," he said, "I profited by a negative example."

"You've taken good care of Mom."

"Somebody had to."

"And me. You've taken care of me."

"And that's where I've failed." He sat there trying not to move.

"But you've got Mimi back," I said. "She's not going anywhere. And you haven't screwed around on her. You've been a better husband to Mimi than Dad ever was to Mom."

"Well, I hope so," he said.

"So," I said, "what the hell were you doing in my room?"

"Stop it, Denny. Why do you do this to yourself." He was looking around at the walls.

"Why? Why do I travel? Why do I leave my body? Why did that get to be a habit? Elliot, I think I have you to thank for that."

He was trying not to listen. "You ever wonder why these places are green?"

"Because grass is green," I said. "Look at me, God damn it."

"I'm listening. The more I listen, the less I understand you, frankly. I know you're going through the tortures of the damned—"

"There were two shots, right?"

"That's right," said Elliot. He was holding himself steady. I could see his hand through the tabletop, massaging the side of his knee.

"I know why he botched the first one, Elliot."

"Why?"

"He didn't want to die."

Elliot sighed. "Oh, Denny," he said.

"Don't oh Denny me. I remember his face. I remember the gun on the floor. He didn't try to reach it."

I saw Elliot blink. "You went back in time, is that it?"

"I was there! I lived through it too!"

He shot a glance toward the guard. "Denny, take it easy—"

"He knew Mom would never really leave him. If he hurt himself, maybe she'd forgive him. She loved him. They loved each other. I'll tell you what I still can't remember, though. You actually picking up the gun. It was on the floor, Dad was asking me for help—Elliot, did you make *me* pick it up?''

He looked in his lap. ''Denny, I hope you realize you're babbling—''

''I can hear myself, yes. What was going through your mind? You put your finger around his finger and you pulled the trigger, how exactly did that feel?''

''Whoa,'' said Elliot. ''Listen to yourself.''

''That's all I ever do, Elliot. Except when I listened to you. Sit down!'' I shouted.

He froze halfway out of his seat. Then he sat down again, slowly.

''You knew I didn't see you do it. The night you killed him, that was the first time I left my body—you didn't know exactly what was happening but you saw how dazed I was, you knew you could fuck with me, plant any bullshit memory, I'd believe it. Except now you had to watch over me, make sure I didn't remember the truth. Not that you didn't love me, Elliot, I'm sure you did, I'm sure you still do in your way—''

''Denny? Press Stop.''

''—You loved me like a father. Wasn't easy raising me, either. I was flaky. I did things I didn't remember. When I went to prison the first time, it kind of broke your heart. Of course in the meantime you met Mimi, that changed the equation. Now you had something else Dad never had, a wife you loved and cherished, a wife you were faithful to. Things started to look up for the first time in your life—then boom, I get my parole. You had to take me in, because of course you believe in family, that's the star you steer by, if you ignore your family you're no better than Dad. Then Gwen Lefcourt comes along. Starts leading me back down the road to ruin. Mimi leaves you.

You go nuts. It's all happening again. Now you're *really* like Dad, you don't know *who* to kill.''

I heard chairs scraping. The jury was getting ready to leave the jury room. Elliot, too, was on his feet.

"That was you coming out of her house. That was you I saw that night. That was Dad's .38 you took along.''

"I'm leaving,'' said Elliot. He was looking around for the guard.

"You asked her if I was there. I wasn't, but you didn't believe her. You called her a liar, you called her all kinds of names, you threatened her, she told you to go fuck yourself, you put a bullet in her heart. That's when you started to think—two birds with one stone. If I go back to prison, Mimi comes back to you—plus if I hang, I'm out of both your lives forever. That's why you gave Gwen those abrasions, trying to make it look like rape—''

"*Guard*?''

"—and the .38 under the floorboard in my room, hoping the cops would find it. You shouldn't have hidden it so well, you could've saved yourself a lot of legal bills—''

He wheeled on me fiercely. "If there's a gun in your room, it's because *you* put it there—''

"—Trouble was, it didn't have my fingerprints—''

"—just like you hid the liquor in Mimi's drawer so I could find it, don't you understand?''

"Yeah, I get it, asshole, you're still trying to fuck with me. Hey look, what did I expect—''

"Mr. Hake?''

Elliot and I both looked around. The bailiff was at the door.

"Jury's back,'' he said.

I got up slowly, baring my teeth at Elliot. The

bailiff led me out into the hallway. I could see the panic in his eyes.

"God help you," he said. Before I knew it, he was halfway to the elevator. I took my seat in the courtroom. Jordy was looking around for Elliot.

"He's gone," I started to say, but then there he was at the door, peering in coldly through the square of glass. The jury was back in the box, the foreman was conferring with the bailiff. I saw Mom with her head down, in the front row. The foreman stood up. Though I knew what he was going to say, I couldn't help murmuring an angry little prayer, precisely what I don't remember. My soul flew up toward the ceiling. Below, I saw Mom rise up out of her chair and I heard a shriek of pain come out of her mouth. She was still crying when the bailiff led me out.

14

After sentencing they moved me to C wing. The noise on the Row was like nothing I'd ever heard, the screams, the groans, the constant hollering about changing the TV channel—the sets were hung just outside the cells, on the other side of the light bulbs, so at night what you saw was a light bulb with some motion behind it, which seemed to focus everybody's anger. Every morning they passed out safety razors, which they collected a half hour later. My suicide watch was off—as far as I could tell, nobody on death row was under observation, though people were constantly finding ways to cut themselves, but in any case I felt completely calm. The heat, the noise, were intense, but I had never felt so empty, so concentrated, like a laser beam sweeping a cave. I kept replaying the two memories, Elliot curling his finger around Dad's, Elliot walking out of Gwen's house the night she was murdered. When I tried to travel I didn't get far, and the farther I tried to go the dimmer everything got, like some new physical law was governing my efforts. The first night after they moved me, I did see the three of them at Elliot's— Mimi, Elliot, and Mom—then Mom at home, sitting on the cellar steps, staring into the gloom, and Elliot in his backyard, asleep on the patio or tossing horseshoes by himself in the twilight. Later Elliot and Mimi started going out every night, usually coming home drunk—either Elliot had given up on the idea of children, or they were adopting after all. I could tell that foster child a thing or two, was my thought.

In the first days they took me alone to the showers—though the hall porters were playing it down, there was a story going around that I'd ratted out Carl Williams after all. That rumor seemed to die its own death, because later on I went with the group. Nobody hassled me, nobody talked to me. I didn't care. I wasn't feeling much of anything, and seeing what rage did to people on the Row, I didn't want to give in to it just yet. I was waiting to talk to Randy, who was off at some convention, meanwhile trying to keep an eye on Elliot without letting my fury get the better of me. Also, the Row was full of crazies, and I had to keep my wits about me. One guy in particular was working himself up to talk to me—I could sense it every time we went to volleyball.

One day, along about the third week, he sat down on the bench next to me. Across a room he could have passed for a teenager, but up close I saw the wrinkles in his eyes.

"I know who you are," he informed me, as if I'd been concealing it from him and him alone. "You're that guy killed his wife when he was someplace else."

I didn't answer and he didn't press me. Weird pauses were tolerated here, as if everybody had the option of hoarding their energy, guarding their life force. I sat listening to the thunk of the volleyball game. The net was made of chain, fastened to the walls with earthquake bolts, and the ceiling of the cage was so low half the shots bounced off it. "I was never married and I didn't kill anybody," I said at last. I could hear the listlessness in my voice, and the finality, and that frightened me.

"Yeah, welcome to the club," he said.

"I'm not in any club," I said. I was trying to picture Elliot, and all I could see was Mimi sunning herself on the patio. Ozzie was chasing a squirrel, yellow light was pouring through the trees, and suddenly my arm was bleeding. The guy had cut me with a toothbrush—there was a razor blade melted into the handle, and my blood was running down onto the floor. I stared at the drops, one by one.

"Fuck you do that for," I said. I looked up and saw a guard leading him casually out the door, both of them smiling back at me. I showed my arm to a second guard, and he took me to the infirmary, sprayed my upper arm with germicide, wrapped it, and took me back to my cell. All along the run, guys were heckling me. So the rumor about Carl was alive after all, or maybe I was being targeted for having my face in the tabloids—OUT OF BODY AT THE TIME. Either way I didn't care. "I want to talk to Randy Nelson," I said to the guard. "Could you tell me when I can do that?"

He went away and came back.

"Your privileges didn't come through yet."

"When do I get phone privileges?"

"In the next world," he said.

"Come back here," I said.

"Don't fuck with me, dead man."

"Just tell me this. Has Randy Nelson tried to call me?"

The guard walked away without answering. I

couldn't blame him, I had nothing to offer him. Then I heard somebody calling my name.

"Hake?"

For a second I didn't know where the voice was coming from, then I realized it was the guy from the next cell. Out of politeness more than anything I drifted out and parked myself behind him. He had his mirror poking out between the bars and he was trying to see me, but my body was on the bed, beyond his view.

"You getting used to it yet?" he said.

I didn't answer. I was trying to picture Randy.

"Fucks with your eyesight, don't it? When they don't let you see distances. We had a guy here two years ago, he was so fat when they opened the trap-door it tore his head clean off his body."

"Is that so."

"The family sued."

I watched him put the mirror back in his shirt pocket. "You're behind me, aren't you," he said. "You can see every move I make."

"Yeah, I'm behind you," I heard myself say. A hot cart was going up the run—one of the wing tenders was handing out the evening meal.

"What do I look like?" he said eagerly.

I could only see him hazily—I was staring at the ceiling of my cell. Guards were shining flashlights in. "You got initials carved in the back of your head," I said.

"Yeah, what initials?"

"I don't know. I can't make it out. Something with a C." I heard him grunt—I didn't know if I was close or not, and I didn't care. The porter came and collected the trays. Another guy came and mopped up the run—some of the crazies had tossed their food out the bars. I fell asleep and saw Mom crying, sitting with the fridge door open. There were ants running along the baseboard of her kitchen, all the way to the cat dish. I looked for her again and she was in the living room, watching local news. I started to get emotional, thinking about all the things I'd never see or do again, how all my life had been nothing but a losing battle, then imagining the rope around my neck and cursing my brother with my last breath. I called for the guard.

"I need to make a phone call," I told him. It was a different guard this time.

He went away and came back. "No dice."

"That's bullshit," I said. "Listen. Sooner or later my lawyer is gonna show up, and I'm gonna tell him you didn't let me make a phone call, and that's gonna be a lot of paperwork for you, so why don't we make this easy on both of us."

"I happen to know your lawyer's gone back to St. Louis," he said.

"What do you want in return?"

"Blow me."

I looked him dead in the eye. "All right," I said.

For a second he didn't move—then he let out an uneasy laugh and vanished. The cells went dark and I fell asleep. I could see Elliot in his bed, his arm flung across Mimi's body. My cell door opened, and the next thing I knew two guys were banging on my head with rubber truncheons. I watched them from above, not feeling a thing. Daylight crept through the bars. Breakfast came and went. I heard shouts going up and down the run—people were scrambling in their cells, a guard was beating on the bars. "Woman on the wing," I heard him call.

It was Randy. They were trying to decide whether

to make me talk to her through the bars of my cell. Finally they led her away and then came and slapped some shackles on me and took me to a room divided in two by a fine-mesh screen. You couldn't get a cigarette through, much less a finger, so we didn't shake hands. I didn't feel relieved to see her, I wasn't permitting myself any emotions, let alone hopeful ones—I was waiting to see what she would say.

"Did you get my letter?" I said.

"Yes," she said. I was watching us from across the room. "How are you feeling?"

"With my fingers," I said.

She understood. "It must be hideous."

"Everything I told you was true."

She nodded once, slowly.

"That day on the boat? You and your friend? Could you tell I was listening?"

She didn't say anything. She closed her eyes. "Yes," she said. "I could tell."

Thank God, I thought. "Randy," I said, "he killed my dad. He's been living with that guilt for twenty years. Or maybe he doesn't feel guilty, I don't know. Assisted suicide, maybe that's how he looks at it. Maybe he thinks of himself as a hero, all I know is he fucked me good."

She winced. She must have been thinking about my polygraph, or how she was willing to go along with the insanity plea, because she said, "And me, too."

I felt myself relax a notch. "Help me," I said.

"I want to."

"I know you do," I said.

"What can we prove?"

"Randy, I saw my brother in my room. I saw him lift up the floorboard. The gun is there, a .38 caliber revolver, I know it." For an instant I glimpsed Elliot zonked out on his patio, and my heart filled with loathing. I could taste my frustration and Randy's too.

"Tell me what to do," she said.

"See, I don't think he's totally cold-blooded. I think his mind is divided."

She smiled faintly. "Runs in the family."

"Yes. Exactly." My hands were on the mesh. "He was trying to protect me. And get rid of me. And rescue his marriage, all in one neat bundle, and he succeeded, I've been seeing them at the house, they're back together, happy as clams."

She was nodding. "He may not even remember he did it," she said.

I frowned. "You think so?"

"Given your family history. It could be as hazy as a dream to him."

"Or it could be eating him alive," I said.

"That's also possible," she said. "I'm just trying to think of your avenues of appeal—"

"Randy, *he* hired my lawyer, the worst one he could find—the killer paid my lawyer, that's gotta be grounds for reversal. Have you spoken to Simon Lefcourt?"

Randy shook her head. "He hasn't returned my calls."

"Why? Has he decided I did it?"

She didn't answer. I tried to picture Lefcourt, but I couldn't. "I think he's confused. I think he cares about you, I know he does—"

"But not like you do."

She glanced down shyly—grateful, I guess, that I bore her no grudge. "We could try and locate his private detective."

"Yes," I said eagerly. "Get out to the house, pry up that floorboard, do the ballistics."

She nodded. "Are you keeping an eye on Elliot?"

"I'm trying," I said. "Randy, it's hard. Now that I know what makes me tick, I can't tick. I'm numb. It's like living on a cancer ward."

"I'll do everything I can," she said. She put her hand up to the mesh.

"I know you will," I said. Our fingers were barely touching—suddenly I saw the guard grab me by the shoulders, shove me back into my chair. Randy started to object, but they were hustling her out of there, and the next thing I knew she was out in the corridor, arguing with the guard, demanding to talk to his superior—meanwhile they were shuffling me back down the run. The kid who cut me with the toothbrush leaped to the bars.

"Hey. You gonna fly into my cell and kill me?"

I didn't even look at him. I was trying to follow Randy, see if she'd made any headway with the guard, but everything was gray. The next thing I knew I was in my cell on my back. As far as I could tell, it was next morning.

"Was that your lawyer came yesterday?" said the guy next door.

"No," I heard myself say. "My therapist."

"Your therapist! Man, your ass is down for sure. You get your date yet?"

"No."

"Bullshit. I heard you were going in July."

I rubbed my eyes. How far off was July? I was still trying to find Randy, but I couldn't move, I couldn't see myself, couldn't see anything, I was trapped. And sure enough, now the walls started to close in like a vise. I must have started screaming, because my cell door was open and two guys were taking whacks at me again. Then they were gone. My arms were covered with bruises. The guy in the next cell, the guy with the initials in his head, was rattling away.

"Next time you travel, could you do me a favor? If I give you my lawyer's address? Tell him I need some false teeth, the warden won't let me have them."

The cell door opened again, the same two guys. They snapped on the shackles and led me down the hallway. Focus, I thought. Then another door opened and I was in the barber shop.

"You think you're fucking Jesus, don't you."

It was the kid who had cut me. He had one hand behind his back. I looked around for the barber, for the guard, but we were locked in there alone.

"Jesus was a faggot," he said.

"Yeah, fine," I said.

"You got any children?"

"No," I said.

"Neither did Jesus. You fucking snitch," he said. He made a lunge for me. I grabbed his arm, the toothbrush dropped to the floor, and I kicked it away. Next thing I knew I was slamming his head into the floor, not watching myself do it, doing it, until the door burst open and two guards came rushing in. One snatched up the toothbrush, the other started beating on my body with a club, while a third guard came and led the kid away, throwing him a look of contempt, like they'd invited this guy to take me out and he'd blown it but they were willing to give him one more chance.

It's over, I thought. I can't see a thing. I'm dead.

"Hake," said the guard—they were leading me

back to my cell by a belly chain, ''you're never gonna see your date, you know that?''

I didn't say anything. He hit me one for good measure and shoved me back in my cell. I lay there drifting up and down the walls and across the ceiling and down again, unable to get any farther than that, thinking, this is what I get for dredging up the past, I can't move, I can't see, I'm powerless. I started pounding on the wall, first my fist, then my head, banging away, just another nutcase on death row, that's all I was ever meant to be, I saw that now, it was all make-believe, my gift, my mobility, total fucking bullshit. I screamed for the guard.

Two of them came trotting down the run.

''I want to see the chaplain.''

''What do you want to see him for?''

''I want my date moved up.'' I sounded like I meant it and I didn't care.

''Why, you got a bet down?'' They went away laughing. I lay down on the bed, trying to see something, drawing a blank, not even trying. It was all a fog.

I heard my cell door clank open. I covered my head with my elbows. I heard footsteps ease in, and when I peeked out from between my arms I saw a gray-haired young guy in a short-sleeved shirt and neatly creased blue jeans.

''You asked to see the chaplain.''

''Are you him?''

''Bob Regan,'' he said, and put out his hand. I sat up on my bed. His face was a blur. ''What's this all about?'' he said.

I closed my eyes. The blur was still there. ''I'm supposed to be getting a new lawyer. My therapist was here, I haven't heard from her in days.'' Days?

I was trying to peer through him, and for a second I could. I saw Randy at a table in a restaurant, drinking coffee.

"We have a unit psychiatrist comes once a month. If you'd like to talk to him, I'll be happy to put you on the list."

"Quit patronizing me," I said. Randy was gone and he was back. "What did you say your name was?"

"Bob Regan," he said. "Where did you get those bruises?"

He was looking at my arms. "Let me ask you something, Bob. What's the difference between the spirit and the soul?"

"Yes, I noticed you have a Bible in here."

"You know where that Bible came from?"

"No," he said carefully, "I don't."

"The Sands Hotel, Las Vegas. My mom, who is not a vicious woman, smuggled it out in her suitcase, though, as you can see, the sticker says Do Not Remove. Does that mean her soul is defective?"

The chaplain's eyebrows started to twitch, like he was trying to remember some lesson from the seminary. "The soul," he said, "is the seat of the passions. The spirit houses the higher affections. And the Devil drives his wedge between the two."

"I see," I frowned. "And after death? Our souls are with God, but not our bodies?" I could hear Randy's voice now, and her friend's voice, the woman from the sailboat, across the table, but their words were drowned in the restaurant clatter. "Where does the spirit of Jesus come into it?"

"The Holy Ghost, you mean?"

"The Holy Ghost keeps you from evil, is that how it works?"

He smiled uneasily. "Roughly, yes."

Now Randy's friend had her hand on Randy's wrist. Don't do it, she was saying. "How familiar are you with my case?"

"Somewhat familiar," he said.

I touched the chaplain's arm. "Will you call my therapist for me?"

"Well, I'm afraid I can't do that—"

"See, the thing is, Bob, I'm going insane. I didn't plead it at my trial but it's happening. I'm starting to think I'm guilty, I'm losing faith. There's a guy here on the Row, they're gonna let him have his way with me—"

"God will protect you. If you ask Him."

"Simple as that?" I said.

"Simple as that," he said. He didn't blink. He meant it. I was hanging by a thread, but that thread was made of steel. That's what he was saying. "It will help if you pray aloud," he said gently.

"All right," I said. Randy was putting on her coat. Her friend got up, too, to stop her. Randy kissed her on the cheek and bolted out the restaurant door. I was trying to follow, but the fog closed in again.

"Will praying aloud embarrass you?" said the chaplain.

"Yes," I said. "But if you think that's what God wants."

"I'll leave if you want me to," he said.

"No," I said. I was losing Randy. "If I can't pray in another man's presence, that means I'm ashamed of my faith. Which means I'm on the side of the Devil."

"If you want to look at it that way," he said. He was enjoying this little discussion, like I was a cross-word puzzle he was filling in. A bell was tolling on another wing. I saw Randy get into her blue Honda.

"God," I said, "I'm sorry . . ."

I was trying to make my mouth move, but it was like trying to talk in the middle of a dream. "Sorry for what?" said the chaplain. He was nodding at me, urging me to go on, but all I could see was Randy. Her Honda was climbing a hill, the back road to Elliot's house. "Sorry for what, Denton?"

Pines flowed past. My heart was in my throat and I forced myself to speak.

"Sorry for the pain I've caused others. And sorrier for the pain I don't know about."

"How do you mean that?" he asked.

I was floating over Elliot's, over the backyard, over the driveway. Elliot's Camry was gone and he was nowhere in the house.

"Denton, did you hear me? What pain?"

I saw Randy's Honda pull to the curb, and I heard my own voice.

"I've done some things, and I've buried my head in the sand. My life trained me to do that, but that's no excuse. I'm not a trained seal. I'm a human being."

"Go on."

Randy was getting out of her car. "I can't go on. Don't torture me."

"You feel God is torturing you?"

"No. Yes."

"Why?"

"Not knowing what I did. Not knowing what I am."

I was shaking. The chaplain gripped my hand. I saw him put his arm around me and I could see him and Randy, too. She was peering in the front window.

"Randy!" I cried suddenly.

"Who is Randy?" said the chaplain.

I saw Randy pull back from the window.

"—It's in the garage," I heard myself say.

"That's where what is?" said the chaplain. My whole body was trembling. Randy was making her way up the driveway, checking her watch, glancing back over her shoulder at the street.

"God, be careful," I heard myself say.

"Take it easy, Denton. God's not angry. God doesn't want you to feel crazy. God understands—"

"*You* don't understand." A bell was ringing close by, and Elliot's Camry was coming up the hill. The chaplain was standing up. "Where are you going? Listen to me—" I said, but now Randy was trying the garage door. It was locked. I saw her open her bag and take out her wallet, searching for a credit card, and then slip a card into the lock. "No!" I cried.

Elliot's car was pulling up in front of the house.

"Denton, I'll be back after your recreation."

"Randy!"

She backed away from the garage. Elliot was coming up the walk—suddenly he stopped to listen. I saw Randy drop the credit card back in her bag and start back down the driveway, skidding to a stop as Elliot rounded the corner. She was backing away from him.

"—and I *am* going to speak to the psychiatrist—"

"God damn it," I said. "Listen to me. My therapist's in danger. She's at my brother's house, you've got to get somebody out there." Elliot was opening the back door, stepping aside to let her enter. Now he was pointing to the living room. I saw her sit down—Elliot was still in the kitchen. I saw him open the fridge and take a handful of ice from the freezer and drop in into a glass. Then he just stood there. He leaned his forehead against the refrigerator door. His fists were clenched. His face was gray.

"Oh God," I said. "Oh no."

He was going out the back door. Randy hadn't moved, and I was pacing, the chaplain with his arm around me, telling me to take it easy. I saw Elliot cross the lawn to the garage, pause at the door and take out his keys, glancing back at the house. Randy was looking at her watch and now Elliot was going up the stairway to my room. I grabbed the chaplain's sleeve.

"Call the police." I could barely hear my voice. Elliot was prying up the floorboard and Randy was still sitting there.

"—in the name of the Father and the Son and the Holy Ghost, amen." The chaplain stood up. Randy was returning to the living room. I looked around the cell and the chaplain was gone. The bell was still ringing.

"One through seven to recreation."

"I don't need any volleyball." My tongue was thick. Elliot picked up the revolver. The kid with the toothbrush came out of his cell.

"Fucking headcase."

He was right behind me—we were both in leg irons. A door slammed and the shackles came off.

"You're up, faggot." The toothbrush kid was breathing in my face. I saw Elliot tuck Dad's revolver in his waistband and start back for the main house.

"Elliot, no!"

"Who's Elliot?"

"Randy!"

"Leave him alone. He's way gone."

"Hey, freako, pretend you're awake."

"Your serve, three-seven."

"Go," I said to Randy.

"You're the one with the ball, dickwit."

Randy was sitting in the living room, Elliot was coming in the back door. Something was yanking at me, like my body had reached out its hands and was trying to snatch me back.

"Watch out," I said.

"You watch out, motherfucker."

Randy stood up.

"Get out of there," I said.

"Hold him," the kid said. "I'm gonna put this boy out of his misery."

"Randy, get out of there!"

"Who the fuck is Randy?"

"Leggo," I said. I swiped at his face. Down he went. "Randy!"

Two guys were holding me. I saw the kid's toothbrush come out—I flailed out, trying to grab him around the neck, watching Elliot stroll back into the kitchen, take the gun out of his belt, then stop in his tracks. He was writing something out on a post-it, sticking it to the fridge. I screamed Randy's name again, two, three times—suddenly she was running across the living room. I saw her turn and pull open the door and run up the sidewalk, Elliot behind her, gun in hand, staring through the open door at Randy fleeing toward her car. I saw Elliot walk into the hallway, look out at Randy, and cock the revolver. I felt something puncture my arm.

"Elliot!"

He had the gun to his head. My mouth was in his ear and my hands were around the kid's neck, squeezing.

"No!" I screamed into his face. "You hear me,

you know ỹou hear me, Elliot, don't, I forgive you—''

His mouth curled into a smile. He blinked his eyes.
I heard the gun go off.

''Jesus God—''

His body crumpled.

''No!'' I screamed. ''Elliot!'' Blood was pooling
out beneath his head. I dug my fingers into his face
and they pulled me off the kid, the chaplain and two
guards and the hospital attendant, hustling me down
a hallway through a sliding gate. My arm throbbed
where the hypodermic needle had gone in. I fell back
on a bed, not my cot, clean sheets. How much time
had passed I couldn't tell, but the house was full of
cops and technicians, all stepping aside to let Mimi
through.

''—Denton, can you hear me?''

It was Randy's voice.

I looked around Elliot's living room, but she
wasn't there. Then I saw her face looming above
mine.

Elliot's body was lying in the hallway and they
were covering it with a blanket.

I closed my eyes.

''He's dead,'' I said.

''Yes,'' said Randy. She was there by my bed.

''He shot himself. My brother shot himself.''

''Yes,'' she said gently. ''I know.''

''With Dad's gun.'' The fog was rolling in again.
My eyes were tearing up. ''He shot himself with my
dad's gun.''

''That's right,'' said Randy. ''Easy does it, don't
try and get up.''

I sank back on the pillow. The fog was making it
hard to breathe. ''That's the gun that killed Gwen.

It's my dad's .38 revolver. I never touched that gun, my prints aren't on that gun.''

"Yes," she said. "They understand."

I opened my eyes. "Did you hear me tell you to get out?"

She nodded tightly. "What's happening now?" she said.

"They're bagging the note. He left a note, he stuck it to the fridge." My head was furry with sedative, tears blurred my eyes.

"Do you know what it says?" said Randy.

I tried to picture the post-it. DENNY, I saw, TELL DENNY. "He made a confession," I said.

"That's right," said Randy.

They had the sheet of paper, now they were looking through his closet. "The shoeprints on Gwen's carpet. They came from his shoes."

"Yes," said Randy.

"He told them everything."

"And Denny?"

I could still see the post-it. TELL DENNY I'M SORRY, it said. "What?" I said.

"He made a new will. He made you his beneficiary."

"Oh Jesus," I said. Elliot! A sick feeling gripped my heart. "I thought he was going to kill you. I warned you and you heard me."

"Yes," she said. There was a doctor in the room and he was taking my pulse.

"Why did you go there alone, that was crazy."

"He wasn't supposed to be there," she said. "I made a date to meet him for coffee."

"He didn't believe you."

"I guess not," she said.

"He knew you believed me."

"I guess so."

"And I was there," I said. "You heard me. What did it sound like?"

"Like a voice in my head. A voice in a dream." Then she said something else, I couldn't hear it. I was drowning in sedative again.

"—I've already spoken to Simon. Denton, can you hear me?"

"Yes," I said thickly. Doctors were moving around the room.

"He's getting you a new lawyer."

"Thank you," I said. "Thank you, Randy." I was fading fast.

"—Denton?"

"Yes. I'm here."

"They're asking me to go."

"Will I see you again?"

"Whenever you want."

The air brightened. My body felt heavy. "And bring your girlfriend. I'd like to meet her face to face."

She smiled at that. "We'll all go sailing."

"Good enough," I said. I lay staring at the ceiling, and through it to the blazing sky.

"Goodbye," I said.

Then the room went out like a light.

15

I was there in person when they put him in the ground. Mimi agreed to delay the funeral until my situation clarified—at first the D.A. wasn't going to let me out, because of the charges pending against me for aiding and abetting Carl Williams in his flight from justice, but then Simon Lefcourt's lawyer worked out a compromise: they agreed to drop the charges but reinstated my parole. There was no mention of the Fay's Big & Tall burglary, none at all. It was hard, then it was easy.

At Mom's insistence, Elliot was buried next to Dad. They didn't ask my opinion, and I didn't offer it.

"Just don't bury me between them," I said to Mom.

She seemed to be having trouble grieving, as was Mimi. I was being allowed my quota of bitterness, which I was being careful not to use up all at once. A light rain was falling. The cemetery was full of hills, and would have been a nice soothing green except for the headstones. There was no service, no eulogy, and the minister read the usual stuff from the Book of Common Prayer, per my instructions. Dust to dust, and so forth, in the midst of life we are in death, and when I heard those particular words I had my first gentle thoughts, a memory of me and Elliot hanging out on our street, riding our bikes, just a quick breeze of nostalgia but it was enough to open the floodgates. For a second I was drifting over water, floating past the table where Gwen and I first had lunch. I took off my sunglasses, wiped away my tears. Mom was watching me. Perhaps I was crying for her benefit.

After it was over, and we were returning to our cars, I went over to Mimi to thank her. There were some media there, stragglers—most of the tabloids had lost interest after it became clear I wasn't going to hang, but there were enough cameras around to spook her. She had refused all interviews—not that she didn't need the money.

"You were watching, weren't you," Mimi said.

"When?"

"That night I was drinking when I shouldn't have been. I was supposed to be quitting. You saw my hiding place."

I shrugged. I was through talking about this. If she wanted to believe, that was her business.

"I guess I can tell you," she said. "I feel lucky he didn't come after me."

I hadn't looked at it like that. "His mind wasn't right, that's for sure," I said.

"No," she said. I had the creepiest feeling she was going to ask me to move from the garage into the main house—then I remembered the house was already listed.

"The thought of losing you," I said, "made him lose control." That sounded lame, like I was blaming her, so I added, "And I was the thorn in his side. The root of all the evil in his life."

"Never in mine," she assured me.

"Plus the memory of our dad," I said.

"Maybe his mind didn't do it," she said. "Maybe his body was responsible."

"Uh-huh," I said. I could tell she didn't really mean this, she was hunting for some answer she could carry around until it wore thin. By that time so would her memory of Elliot.

"He was jealous of you," she said.

"Was he." She didn't sound like she believed this either.

"And he always took care of you. Even in death, leaving you everything."

This was what she wanted to discuss.

"He never signed the new will," I said. "It was never notarized." So I was telling her not to worry, I wasn't going to try and get Elliot's money, what little there was left.

"You're a good man, Denton. I'm sorry I misjudged you."

I let it go. "Some family you married into," I said. She leaned over and pressed my hand, more or less the way she'd done that time in her living room. God, I thought suddenly, if I'd taken her up on that, Elliot probably would have killed her, too. But I didn't dwell on this idea. I gave her a light hug, got into my Camaro. I had half a mind to drive to Randy's office, but then I remembered it was a Sunday, Randy's day to go sailing, so I followed Mom back to her place. There were media trucks up and down the block and strange cars in front of the house. I waited until the media were all packed up and the cars gone, then went around the block and came in the back way. Mom had an afterglow in her eyes and I realized she'd been giving an interview.

"What did you tell them?"

She was defensive. "Denton, we've got bills."

"We'll get them paid. At least I don't have to rob anyone this time."

"Please," she said.

"And remind me to fetch your Bible when I go by the house." I couldn't help zinging her—where was Mom when Elliot was stage-managing my trial? If she'd had an inkling of what he was up to, she certainly hid it from herself. But it was useless to start resenting her, when I'd been so fond of her so long.

"They interviewed Sandra Loyacano, too," she said. "She came clean. Said she invited you inside."

"Nice of her," I said.

"I knew you never harmed that girl. They paid her fifteen hundred dollars."

"Well," I said ruefully, "so we're all making out on this."

She tapped my hand with her finger. "God doesn't want us to be spiteful."

"I'm glad you still know what God wants," I said. Then I realized she was mostly talking to herself. "Just don't let this drive *you* crazy, okay?"

"Well, I'll try," she said. "There's still some stuff in the basement, could you help bring it up?"

I went down to the cellar, started hauling up cartons of Dad's old hobby magazines. It was the first time I'd been in the cellar, in the flesh that is, since the day he died. I looked around at his workbench, the place where I pictured him lying, but all it was now was cold cement. Beyond was a door, with pencil lines on it, and dates above the pencil lines—the door where Dad used to measure our heights every Christmas, one column of lines marked ELLIOT, the other marked DENTON. There was a two-inch space between Elliot age 14 and Elliot age 15 and of course nothing above that. He'd had a growth spurt that last year.

"I'm taking the empties," I said, when I got upstairs with the last carton. "I'll see you in a few days, okay?"

"Why, where are you running to now?"

"Walla Walla," I told her. "Got a meeting at the prison."

"No. Denny, why?"

"Least I can do. They accepted Simon's bid, he asked me to put in my two cents. He's wondering if I'll show up on time—keeps looking at his watch. And I gotta go pick up my stuff, Mimi's showing the house to some people."

"You can see them, can you? In your mind's eye?"

"Sure. Down to the nicotine stains on her fingers." In truth, all I could see was a woman strolling through Elliot's backyard. "Mom, I'm kidding. It's all nonsense, I just went bonkers for a while. I've got an overactive imagination, you always said so."

"That's right, blame it on me." She squeezed my arm as I headed for the door. "Denny, you know I always tried my best."

"I know, Mom. Me too. We'll be all right." I hugged her, feeling her go frail in my arms—she was starting to cry. I still felt tempted to say something about what happened the night Dad shot himself, how she'd never said a word about Dad calling out for help, but I didn't want to leave on a sour note. I got into my car, drove to Elliot's. There was a realtor's sign on the lawn, but no buyers in sight, no sign of Mimi or any other woman in the backyard. I hurried up to my room, transferred my clothes into the empty cartons, threw in Mom's Gideon Bible and her plastic mosaics, and carried my TV out to the Camaro.

As I slammed down the trunk, Randy's blue Honda pulled up behind me. That's who I'd seen in Elliot's backyard—I had hoped it was Randy.

"I passed you on the way out," she said. "I was just here."

"I saw you," I said. She walked with me back to the garage to get the cartons.

"The garage was open. I left you a note. I tried to call, but the phone's been disconnected."

"What note? I didn't see it."

"Next to your family pictures?"

I knew I'd forgotten something—the photos Elliot had set out in my room, the one of him with Mom, the one of Mom alone. "What's it say?" I didn't much want to go up there again, even in my mind.

"I was afraid you'd leave town without calling me."

"No. Just clearing out my stuff. Going east for a couple of days."

"Ah," she said. I saw her glance over her shoulder—the house, the yard, they were spooking her, too. "I'm glad," she said.

"Simon's letting me live in one of his condos till I find a place of my own. Why, did you fill my hours?"

She nodded yes. "Did you want me to?"

"Yeah, if you promise not to tell Ortega." I picked up the cartons. "Where's your friend?"

She didn't answer. "I'll tell Ortega you're cured."

"There you go. I thought today was your day to go sailing."

Randy shrugged. "She said she had something to do."

"Trouble in paradise?"

"No." She looked at the ground. "Who knows. Probably."

"Want me to check up on her for you?"

"No, I don't want you to check up on her." And she smiled in spite of herself.

"Easily done. Where is she, on her boat?" I scrunched up my face, pretending to focus. "Oh yeah, there's somebody with her. Whoa, I think it's a guy."

"Denton." She slapped lightly at my arm. If I wasn't mistaken, it was the first time we'd really touched. She frowned behind her smile. "I never thanked you for saving my life," she said.

"Well," I said, "you never really quit on me either."

"That means you have to look after me now."

"Yeah, I've heard that one," I said. We were out front now—I took her hand and looked at it, the way a doctor examines your fingers.

"Your turn to take care of people," said Randy.

"I guess," I said. My voice sounded weary. She started to draw her hand away. I held it. After a moment she squeezed back, hard.

"I'm sorry," she said. Maybe she thought I was still bitter over her not believing me sooner, but I wasn't. I was just feeling exhausted, and with a five-hour drive ahead of me. At the curb she turned and kissed me on the cheek.

"Call me," she said.

"Well, of course," I said.

"You promise?"

"I promise," I said. I watched her get into her

Honda, then loaded the rest of my stuff in the trunk. She followed me down the hill, waving as I peeled off onto I–90. I drove until my eyelids got heavy, somewhere west of Ellensburg, then pulled into a rest stop. My mind went blank, and then I had a stray memory—Dad with his ruler pressing onto my head, barking at me to stop slouching, to stand up tall like a soldier. I pictured him drawing a line on the cellar door and dating it, and then it was Elliot's turn, and then we all went outside and threw a football around, in a cold December drizzle. Finally I got the shivers and Dad tucked me into bed, kissed me and turned off the light. I fell asleep, dreamed I was driving to the future. Then I was.